"Do I get to break?" Lexi asked

"Not literally," Spencer answered with a smile.

Lexi was still laughing when she positioned the ball, then bent over the table, trying to remember how to hold the cue. But she hadn't anticipated the full sexual awareness that would flood through her when Spencer ever so casually leaned over her to correct her position. She shifted slightly, bringing more of him in contact with her body.

"Okay, now shoot," he instructed.

"Do I have to?" She sighed. It looked like all good things must come to an end.

He chuckled, then gently lifted a wisp of her hair away from her face. Tingles zinged down the side of her neck, and sharply pulling the pool cue back, she horribly overcompensated. Lexi heard the "oomph" sound Spencer made when the cue met his stomach—or worse.

"Ohmigosh!" She jerked upright and her head crunched against his.

"Oh…I'm so sorry!" Before she realized what she was doing, she found herself rubbing his stomach about where she judged the cue's point of impact to be.

"Too high." When she moved her hand lower, he inhaled loudly and grabbed her wrist. "Still too high, but thanks for the thought."

Dear Reader,

Season's Greetings! May your holidays be serene, your
gifts elegantly within budget, all toys preassembled, your
home lavishly decorated, your eggnog have plenty of
kick, the extra calories you've eaten magically evaporate,
your dinner guests congenial, your goose perfectly
cooked, and may the dishes be washed by someone else,
preferably your very own Texas man.

But if you find that all is not quite this vision of holiday
perfection, don't despair! Put your feet up, grab a hot
toddy and read the Christmas scenes in *Mr. December.*
You'll definitely feel superior!

Happy Holidays,

Heather MacAllister

Heather MacAllister
MR. DECEMBER

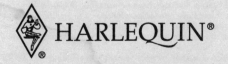

HARLEQUIN®

TORONTO • NEW YORK • LONDON
AMSTERDAM • PARIS • SYDNEY • HAMBURG
STOCKHOLM • ATHENS • TOKYO • MILAN • MADRID
PRAGUE • WARSAW • BUDAPEST • AUCKLAND

With thanks to Christina Dodd,
Jolie Kramer and Jan Freed,
who can be brilliant when they have to be,
and to Susan Macias, whose brilliance we miss.

ISBN 0-373-25811-9

MR. DECEMBER

Copyright © 1998 by Heather W. MacAllister.

Printed in U.S.A.

1

"AND I WAS FEELING so lucky today, too." Lexi Jordan hung up the telephone and erased her mother's message on the answering machine.

She and her roommate, Francesca, had just been booked as the musical entertainment for two private holiday parties at the Wainright Inn next weekend, which meant Lexi could finish her Christmas shopping without maxing out her credit card—enough to put holiday cheer into anyone.

And then her mother had called.

"What's up chez Jordan?" Francesca's voice echoed off the tile in their bathroom, where she was hanging up her underwear to dry.

"Gretchen has a new therapist."

"Your sister always has a new therapist."

"But this one has convinced Mom to gather everyone for Christmas dinner." Lexi wandered from the telephone and stood in the doorway watching her roommate. "She wants me to bring a man."

"Chef? Butler? Entertainment?"

"Significant."

Francesca raised her eyebrows as she unrolled a towel. "Oooh."

Lexi's roommate had an extensive collection of pricey lingerie that required hand washing with a special detergent she ordered from a catalog.

Lexi wore cotton for its breathable qualities.

Once, Francesca had pointed out that silk was also a natural fiber, but Lexi had countered that its breathing quality had been canceled out by the unnatural shapes into which it had been sewn.

"And do you have a significant man I don't know about?"

"I don't even have an insignificant one." Lexi considered the men she knew. Nothing but casual date material. And things were likely to remain the status quo as long as she and Francesca performed at the Wainright Inn in Rocky Falls, Texas on the two hot date nights of the week. "And even if I did find a man, I'd probably alienate him by subjecting him to a family therapy session."

"I thought you said Christmas dinner."

"Did I fail to mention that Gretchen's therapist feels she has unresolved abandonment issues from her childhood?"

"This sounds good. Keep talking." Francesca grinned and picked up a black-and-rose bra from the towel. At least Lexi thought it was a bra. There wasn't a whole lot to identify.

She leaned against the doorjamb. "Well, this woman told Gretchen that our parents were emotionally remote and more interested in the welfare of the arts community than in Gretchen. Can you believe it?"

Francesca met Lexi's eyes in the mirror over the sink. "Kinda."

"Frankie! Get real. Who do you think is paying for Gretchen's therapy? Besides, *I* don't have a problem with my parents."

"Uh…"

Lexi grimaced and waved her hand. "*Other* than the normal stuff. They were around. They spent a lot of time with me, and they always came to my recitals when I was little. They *still* come. They aren't emotionally remote. I could just smack Gretchen."

Francesca hung up more pieces of the black-and-rose set, then fished out a dark swirl of fabric from the sink. "Gretchen is tone-deaf. She can't sing, and she can't play the piano."

"So?"

"So there *weren't* any recitals for your parents to attend. Maybe they did ignore her."

Lexi mentally flipped through her childhood memories of her little sister. "Gretchen's a whiner. She's impossible to ignore." And this latest scheme was an attention-getting ploy if ever Lexi saw one.

Francesca laughed as she squeezed out the dark blob and set it on the edge of the sink. "Why Christmas dinner?"

"Gretchen has no happy childhood memories, so we're supposed to create one for her now."

"Actually, that doesn't sound so awful. I think it's sweet."

Francesca wasn't nearly as much fun when she was being logical. Lexi's personal opinion was that humoring Gretchen only encouraged her. "Not sweet. Mother wants to prove we're a normal, happy, well-adjusted, successful family."

Francesca snickered. "Which one is she trying for?"

Lexi drew a deep breath. "All of them. I tried to convince her to abandon the adjectives and just concentrate on the family part, but she insisted. And get this—Les is coming."

Francesca whirled around and knocked the tan-and-black-striped lump back into the water. "Your brother? The gray sheep?"

That was better. They both dissolved into laughter. Lexi's twin brother's rebellions were varied, and short-lived. "Poor Les. He wants to be a black sheep so bad, but every time he comes home, he gets bleached."

"I can't believe your mother managed to get him to come home for Christmas."

Lexi could. "She's got me looking for a date, hasn't she?"

"I don't get it. Why?"

"Because Gretchen's a mess and Mom's afraid who Les might bring."

Francesca gave her a long-suffering look. "Because I am your very best friend...he could bring me."

"Thanks for the sacrifice, but wrong gender."

"No way!"

"Way. At least that's what he said last time he called."

"He probably just said that to get back at your parents for naming him Leslie."

That's what Lexi thought. "Well, it worked."

"I guess *so.*" Francesca scooped out the underwear and let it drip. "But what I really meant was why does it matter if you have a date or not? It's supposed to be a family dinner, right?"

And that was the problem. This time, *family* would include Lexi's Aunt Carolyn, who had, according to Lexi's mother, achieved the perfect life. "I think the date is supposed to steal Aunt Carolyn's thunder on the lack-of-grandchildren issue. She and my uncle, and, it appears, my perfect cousin and her equally perfect husband and children will also be there."

In the mirror, Francesca's eyes widened and she squeezed water down the front of her sweater. *"Emily DeSalvo is coming to Rocky Falls?"*

Did she have to act like it was such a big deal? "So it would seem."

"Oh, my...how can she rearrange her schedule this close to Christmas?"

"That's why she's perfect," Lexi said evenly.

Or maybe not so evenly.

Francesca blinked at her. "Lexi, you're not still jealous of her, are you?"

"I was *never* jealous of her."

"I mean, it'd be okay if you were. She's...she's..." As Lexi's gritted-teeth expression finally registered, Francesca turned back to the sink, obviously deciding to quit while she was ahead.

"She's a world-famous soprano just now reaching her professional peak, while I'm a mere associate professor of piano at a small college in the hinterlands of Texas? Is that what you were about to say?"

There was a short silence. "I wouldn't have said 'hinterlands.'"

Lexi sighed.

"Oh, come on. You can't compare yourself to her."

"Mother does." Lexi half smiled. "You know, I used to accompany Emily at recitals when we were little."

Francesca's eyes brightened. "Was she...I mean, could you tell she was really good back then?"

Lexi nodded. "Yeah. I was no slouch, either, but

once people heard her sing…" She trailed off, re-membering how she'd practice and practice, but Emily's soaring voice would effortlessly eclipse her time and again.

Come to think of it, maybe her parents weren't at the recitals to hear Lexi play after all. Maybe they'd come to hear Emily sing. She frowned.

"Hey."

Lexi discovered Francesca looking at her with a little too much perception.

"We'll have to find you a real hunk for Christmas. Like him." She nodded to the Science Hunks calen-dar hung up beside the mirror.

A bare-chested Santa with an attitude glared at them. And glare was the right description. While most of the men in the calendar had tried for sexy come-ons, this man's expression dared women to take him on.

And Francesca wanted to meet the challenge. She was intrigued with the guy. In the mornings, Lexi could hear her talk to him as she put on her makeup. Lexi admitted that the man had a certain unnerving allure, which hadn't been lessened by the lipstick mouthprint Francesca had left on his cheek.

"There he is, Lexi," she said, making kissing sounds. "A giant piece of male eye candy for Emily to drool over."

Emily wouldn't be the only one. Lexi had gener-ally avoided Mr. December's accusing stare, but that didn't mean she avoided looking at him elsewhere. He had well-shaped hands with long fingers. People in Lexi's profession noticed fingers. Still, she bet she was the only woman who looked past the broad, lightly furred chest, flat stomach and muscled shoulders to notice his fingers.

"What do you think?" Francesca asked, her dimples showing. "He'd be perfect, right?"

"I know it's the season of miracles, but really."

"I keep telling you, it's all a matter of the right underwear."

Lexi stared at the calendar picture. "I have a feeling it'll take more than underwear to nab this guy."

"That's why I wrote to him."

"You didn't!"

Grinning, Francesca retrieved the last of her laundry and drained the water from the sink. "Of course I did. And sent him a picture."

Lexi closed her eyes. "Not the one of you naked with your cello."

"Just to let him know that when I have a fine instrument between my legs, I know how to play it."

"Francesca!"

"You should write to one of those calendar cuties yourself," suggested her unrepentant roommate.

Lexi stared at Mr. December and imagined Emily's envious reaction. Emily envying *her*. What a switch that would be. As Lexi's lips curved in a slow smile, her mother's horrified face popped up in the background, spoiling the fantasy. "I...don't think any of these guys would exactly fit in with my family."

"Not fit in? They're scientists! These guys have brains *and* brawn. Aren't we being just a wee bit picky?"

"Francesca..." How could someone be both savvy and naive at the same time? "That man is no scientist."

"Sure he is!" Francesca rolled the last of her lingerie in a towel. "They all are. They work over at the Electronics Research Facility."

"That white building on the other side of the falls?"

Francesca nodded.

Lexi walked over to the calendar and took it down. Paging through it, she said, "You're telling me that this many smart, single, good-looking guys work just a few miles from here and we've never seen them? I don't think so."

"I was surprised, too, but they were written up in the fall issue of *Texas Men.*"

"So that's why I've seen that thing all over campus." Lexi tacked up the calendar again. "I still think there's a catch somewhere."

"They're all catches."

"You know what I mean." She stared Mr. December right in the eyes. *Was* that intelligence she saw in his gaze? She looked closer. Probably the photographer's umbrella light.

"If you want to read about them, I've got a copy of the magazine." Francesca held up her long, filmy tiger-striped cat suit and draped it over the clothesline hanging above the bathtub. "I sleep with it under my pillow."

Lexi didn't doubt it. Because she knew Francesca expected her to say "no"—certainly not because she was in any way curious about Mr. December—she headed toward Francesca's bedroom. "Under your pillow, you say?"

The magazine was on the nightstand, not under Francesca's pillow, but Lexi presumed that was because she wasn't sleeping at the moment. Lexi had seen this issue of *Texas Men* before—it was hard not to—but she'd only flipped through it, missing the fact that these gorgeous men worked and, therefore, must live within dating range.

She sat on the edge of the bed, smiling when the magazine fell open to Mr. December, or rather *Dr.* December. Yeah, right. "What lucky woman wouldn't like to find Mr. December in her stocking?" she read. In the background, she heard the telephone ring.

"I'll get it!" Francesca warbled. Lexi winced. Her roommate was no soprano.

"Spencer Price, our favorite Santa Claus, holds his doctorate in mechanical engineering.... Lexi stared at Dr. Spencer Price, not certain whether or not she liked knowing his name. It made him more intimidating somehow. And yet, at the same time, it made him human.

She began to think of the possibilities. Here was a man who would speak to her parents on one level, and speak to Emily and Aunt Carolyn on another. No more feeling-sorry-for-Lexi looks. But plenty of jealous-of-Lexi looks.

It was a lovely fantasy—almost as satisfying as the one in which she single-handedly built Littletree College into one of the premier fine arts schools in the Southwest.

And about as likely.

Lexi paged through the magazine and found a 900 number to call for information on how to contact the men.

She was actually contemplating calling when Francesca appeared in the doorway. "Lexi, I can't stand that decrepit building any longer! You know how it was raining this morning?"

Lexi nodded.

"Well, that was Dr. Biersanger's secretary. The leak in the auditorium ceiling finally rotted the acoustic tiles and chunks fell down while the recorder ensemble was on stage."

"Oh, no! Was anybody hurt?"

"No. But they will be unless that place is renovated."

"Renovated?" This was one of Lexi's hot buttons. "Do you know how many potential students and professors have passed Littletree by because of the inadequate number of practice rooms, those aging pianos and the shabby little rehearsal hall?"

"I hear you."

"It's getting so that I'm embarrassed every time we have a guest performer. They should raze the entire building and start again from scratch."

"So why don't you get your father to throw some of his foundation money our way?"

Lexi glared at her. Francesca had just broken the unspoken rule. Lexi's father and his connection to the Cultural Arts Foundation was off-limits.

Sighing, Francesca held up her hands, palms outward. "Sorry. But it's beginning to look like he's our best shot."

Unfortunately, Lexi knew Francesca was only voicing common public opinion around the Littletree music department. Naturally, no one had ever flat-out told Lexi that she'd been hired because she was the daughter of Lawrence Jordan, well-known arts philanthropist, but as the music building deteriorated, there had been a few subtle comments. Then a few not-so-subtle comments.

But she'd really felt the pressure when Dr. Biersanger, the music department chairman, had stopped introducing her as Emily DeSalvo's cousin and started introducing her to prospective students and faculty as Lawrence Jordan's daughter.

Lawrence Jordan their best shot? To Lexi, it looked like he was their only shot. And mainly because she could no longer stand Biersanger's hopeful basset hound expression, she'd already decided to approach her father before the end of the year—but the time, and his mood, had to be right.

"Okay," she told Francesca. "I'm going to ask him."

Francesca raised her fist. "Yes!"

"But you can't tell anybody!"

"Lips sealed." Francesca mimed locking her lips. "But in the meantime my chamber music class has been canceled unless it's all right with you if they rehearse here."

"Yeah, sure."

"I'll call the office back and have them put up a sign, then. Do we have any soft drinks?"

Lexi gave her an innocent look. "Not since we discovered that sodium and bubbles make us bloat."

"I was referring to your secret stash."

Lexi started to deny that she kept an emergency six-pack in her laundry hamper, then admitted, "I drank the last can Monday night while I was grading freshman theory papers."

Francesca grimaced. "I would have cheated then, too," she said as she left.

Lexi stared down at the magazine. Seven available men just a few miles away. And she only needed one. Just one man to please her mother, therefore pleasing her father. One man to reassure Gretchen's therapist. One man to answer Aunt Carolyn's nosy questions. One man to shade her from the brightness of Emily's success.

And maybe one man for her.

Taking the magazine with her, Lexi jumped up and found Francesca arranging chairs around the piano. "Hey, Frankie, do I look okay?" She had on a sweater, in case the heat wasn't working in her studio, a blouse and a long skirt, so she could skip wearing panty hose.

"For what?"

Lexi drew a deep breath and held up *Texas Men*. "I'm going over there—to the research building."

"Now?"

She nodded. "I've got two hours until my next class."

Francesca's mouth opened and closed. "That's what I like about you. When you decide to do something, you go for it. Want to wear my cat suit? I can use the hair dryer on it."

Lexi shook her head. "I'm not wearing that thing. It'll make me uncomfortable."

Francesca gave her a look and spoke in a sultry voice. "It'll keep you on edge."

"I'm feeling edgy already."

"It'll change your body language."

"That's not the language I want to speak."

Francesca rolled her eyes. "If you did, you'd probably get every guy in the calendar to go to Christmas dinner." Eyeing her friend critically, she walked forward and unbuttoned the top two buttons on Lexi's blouse. "Ditch the sweater."

Lexi looked down to where her cleavage would be—if she had cleavage.

"You need a whisper of lace peeking through."

"I don't want my underwear talking for me." Lexi rebuttoned one button and removed her sweater.

Francesca shrugged and finished arranging the chairs for her ensemble class. "There have been occasions when I've been grateful for its...eloquence."

Lexi preferred the more direct approach. Besides, she wasn't fluent in underwear-speak. "Do you always use underwear to get what you want?"

"No. Sometimes I don't wear underwear at all."

"What?" Lexi squeaked.

Francesca laughed as she unfolded the music stands they kept stored in the front closet. "It's usually when I'm playing a concert and the conductor has been a little repressed at rehearsal. Just before we walk on stage for the performance, I whisper in his ear that I'm not wearing underwear. He always gives just a *touch* extra to the concert. Usually speeds up the tempo, too."

"What if the conductor is a woman?"

"Then I make her wear one of my cat suits." Francesca's deep dimples showed. "One size fits all."

Lexi stared at her roommate. "You're making this up."

"Uh-uh." Francesca nodded to a crystal cello figurine on the mantel of the fireplace they never lit because Lexi's grand piano was too close to it. "That's from Martina Golavaskov. In gratitude."

"The *Russian?*"

Francesca arched an eyebrow. "Her reviews got

markedly better after the concert we played together."

"And *you* think it's because of your underwear?"

"Underwear sets my mood," Francesca said. "I love going to those stuffy receptions we have for the symphony donors and wearing lime-green underwear that says Tuesday."

"Aren't you worried that someone will hear it?"

"So what if they do? You need to loosen up, Lexi."

"I'm loose when it counts," she protested. "I just save my emotions for my music instead of wasting them on underwear. Besides, one of us has to stay tight and focused."

"You shouldn't hoard your emotions. Enjoy them. They'll stretch." Francesca smiled slyly. "Just like the cat suit."

Lexi went to hang up her sweater. "I appreciate the offer, but let me try this my way first. What coat should I wear?" she called from the front hall closet.

"Borrow my leather one, but only if you promise to let your hair down."

Lexi grinned. She was already shoving her arms into Francesca's jacket and had every intention of letting her hair down. Standing in front of the hall mirror, she released the tortoiseshell banana clip and shook her head, freeing her waist-length black hair.

Lexi's hair was her one vanity and she coddled it every bit as much as Francesca coddled her lingerie. She was putting on lipstick just as her roommate passed by to get more folding chairs out of the closet.

"If I had hair like that, I could get by with white cotton underwear, too," Francesca said with a sigh, then smiled. "If you see Mr. December, ask him if he got my picture."

Lexi capped her lipstick. "If I see Mr. December, I'm nabbing him for myself."

2

"BUT SHE'S MAD this time."

"Yeah, well, she wasn't exactly cooing in my ear yesterday, either."

"I mean she's *really* mad."

There was a brief silence, then, "Okay. Leave her on hold until I talk to him first."

Spencer Price pretended he couldn't hear the conversation among his research team in the lab outside the walled-off corner generously referred to as his office. He didn't *want* to hear the conversation. He was working on the year-end budget reconciliation, which always put him in a rare bad mood. Everyone on the team knew this, and generally avoided him during budget time.

"You're not going to tell him about the—!" The rest of the panicked sentence was garbled as the speaker was silenced.

"Let me handle this."

Against his will, Spence wondered what "this" was. He contemplated shutting his door, except that he never shut his door, so an assortment of electronic prototype carcasses now propped it open. They were too much trouble to move. Besides, where else would he put them?

Footsteps approached his door. "Hey, Doc?"

Spence glanced up from the computer monitor. "This better be important, Gordon."

His senior research assistant wasn't wearing his customary smile. Not good. "The lady from *Texas Men* magazine is calling. Wait," Gordon warned as Spencer reached for the phone. "There's some... background you should know before you talk to her."

Background? Spencer's mood worsened as he noticed the rest of the team crowding behind Gordon. "What have you done?"

"Told you this was a bad time," muttered someone.

Gordon held up a hand. "You've no doubt noticed the increase in the volume of mail the lab has received since our calendar was featured in *Texas Men*."

An understatement. They both glanced at the canvas mailbag in the corner of Spence's office. "What about it?"

"Some of us—actually, all of us, except you— have been reading the letters, and we've dated a few of the women."

"I know this. The six of you have talked about nothing else for the past three months. You're stalling, Gordon."

"I was hoping she'd hang up."

Everyone looked at the red blinking light on Spencer's phone. "Why?"

Gordon puffed out his cheeks and spread his hands. "She could stand to cool off before she talks to you. When people get themselves all worked up, they tend to say things they regret later."

Spencer eyed him. "Am I going to say something I'll regret later?"

"Probably." Gordon grimaced. "There've been some complaints, okay?"

"Who's been complaining about what?"

"Some of the women we've dated apparently felt we didn't look enough like our calendar pictures and they let *Texas Men* know."

Spencer took a moment to absorb this. Just how many complaints had there been? "Satisfied women don't complain. What did you all do to them?"

A chorus of "Nothing!" answered him.

"Did you ever think that could be the problem?" Spencer turned off his monitor.

"None of them stuck around long enough for us to *do* anything, but I've got the chemistry lab working on—"

"Quiet, Murray." Gordon elbowed him and cleared his throat. "So we got a little carried away with the computer enhancements on the calendar pictures. We're still basically the same people with the same personalities. Right?" He looked around him for agreement.

"Women don't buy those calendars to look at your personality," grumbled the barrel-shaped man in the back.

"But that's all some of us have got."

"News flash. You don't have a personality, Bob."

"Hey!"

"Okay, okay. I've grasped the general problem." Spencer exhaled. "I knew letting a personals magazine run the calendar was a bad idea."

"Just remember how quickly we unloaded the rest of the calendars after they featured us in their fall issue," Gordon pointed out. "Remember the money."

Since securing funds for his robotic hand project occupied most of Spencer's time, it wasn't something he was going to forget. His finger paused over the hold button. "Name and stats."

"Tonya. Blond. Available."

"Thank you." Spencer punched the button and leaned back in his chair. "Tawn-ya," he drawled into the phone, visualizing a blonde at the other end. He wished he could recall a face. "Spencer Price. How have you been?"

"Well, if it isn't Mr. December, himself. I was beginning to think you didn't exist, either."

"Either?"

"First, I get reports that the men in the calendar aren't the same men who show up for dates, and then you won't return my calls or answer my fax."

"What calls?" As he spoke, Spencer watched Gordon sneak over to the stack of papers on the corner of the desk and remove the top third to reveal a nest of pink messages. Spencer snatched at them, fanning them out like a hand of cards. He glared at Gordon, who pointed to the paper beneath the pink slips, which turned out to be the fax.

Gordon and the rest of them scuttled backward out of the room, while Spencer let Tonya blow off steam.

She had every right to be angry that her messages hadn't been acknowledged. What could have been a few minutes of unpleasantness had now become a time-consuming problem.

It was his fault, he silently acknowledged. Since taking on the research manager's position, he'd spent less time researching and more time working on the administrative end. What little time he did find for actually working on the robotic hand project was constantly interrupted. And now he had to turn in the budget.... He remembered insisting that nothing short of disaster should be brought to his attention.

Looks like his team had taken him at his word.

He swiveled his chair toward the wall and the narrow vertical rectangle that passed for a window. Smoothing over the situation was going to require his utmost concentration and all his charm. "Tonya, my assistant just dug your messages out of my inbox. It's a communication problem on this end. He'd been instructed not to interrupt me. My sincere apologies. What can I say?" He smiled, knowing it would sound in his voice. "I've been swamped."

"So have I—with complaints," she snapped, but to Spencer's practiced ears, she didn't sound as angry as before. "Don't any of the rest of them look like their pictures?"

He chuckled lightly—a deliberate move designed to diffuse tension. "It's the centerfold effect. You know these calendars. They're all airbrushing and attitude."

"Dr. Price, let me quote from just a small sampling of the complaints. 'Overweight geek... His ears turned red and he kept staring at my breasts....'" Spencer instantly visualized Bob. He closed his eyes and rubbed the area between his eyebrows.

"'Pasty-white nerd... This egghead had no muscles and obviously has never been in a gym in his entire life.... Creepy... I expected a great-looking tanned guy, with lots of hair who was into parasailing and the hair was supposed to be on his head, not on his back.'"

Spencer interrupted. "Maybe your happy subscribers haven't written in."

"We've been contacting women who've responded to our 900 number. No one is happy. They're requesting refunds. You're costing us money and damaging *Texas Men*'s reputation."

Spencer's financial antenna detected a request for restitution in the offing.

Not a chance.

"It works both ways, Tonya." Her name was Tonya, wasn't it? He'd been working too hard. "There haven't been any love matches on this end, either. You should tighten your screening procedures to keep out the women with unrealistic expectations."

"So you're saying it's unrealistic to expect the other men in the calendar to look on par with you?"

Spencer was trying hard *not* to say that. He was aware that women found him attractive. But since he owed his good looks to fortunate genes rather than any personal effort on his part, he felt no pride. "You flatter me."

"That wasn't my intention, I assure you."

No, her intention was to hold the Rocky Falls-Littletree Electronics Research Facility liable for any financial losses suffered by her magazine. Spencer guessed her publisher had yelled at her, so now she was yelling at him, and he was going to have to figure out a way to appease everybody. Nothing he hadn't done before.

When this whole calendar thing started, it had

been a joke—a spoof on the hunk calendar genre and another crazy moneymaking scheme from Dr. Price's lab. Sure, the guys had enhanced their photos, but they'd never expected anyone to take them seriously until *Texas Men* had called, wanting to feature the calendar.

Obviously, the *Texas Men* readers didn't have a sense of humor.

The truth was, due to the *Texas Men* exposure, so to speak, the calendar had become their largest moneymaker and had funded six months of all-out research on the robotic hand, the project near and dear to Spence's heart. He'd do anything—and pretty much had—to ensure funding for the hand.

If it was the last thing he did, he wanted a working prototype to wave in front of Dr. "Moldy" Oldstein. He wanted to hook the thing up to those arthritic hands and make the guy acknowledge that Spencer Price, the kid he'd said was wasting scholarship money, had been the one to give him back his motility.

At school, Moldy had made his life miserable with his constant insistence that Spencer wasn't doing his best and making him redo designs and projects. Spencer's anger had fueled his determination. Even when he was no longer Moldy's student, the echoes of the man's taunts stayed with him, driving him to succeed.

He'd nearly quit three years ago. He was out of money and out of a job, unless he could get another grant. And who was on the federal grant committee? Moldy Oldstein.

Spencer's eyes sought the framed letter on his wall, as they frequently did when he hit a low point.

He'd memorized the words—they were few enough. "Congratulations. Here's more money for you to waste." The grant had been huge—enough to assemble the crack team here—but the ten-thousand-dollar personal check Moldy had enclosed meant more.

Moldy believed in him—and Spencer realized he always had.

And Tonya thought he'd let her threaten everything he'd ever worked for?

"We need positive feedback to counter the complaints," she was saying.

"The problem could be that the guys don't want to hurt anyone's feelings, so they're dating everyone who responds. I'll see to it that they're more discriminating in the women they choose to contact."

"That's a start. But I need something tangible to show my publisher," Tonya said, confirming Spencer's guess about the situation.

"That's easily solved." He hoped. "We'll ask future dates to send you glowing testimonials. We'll send you engagement announcements. Invite you to the weddings. You'll be godmother to firstborn—"

"I get the picture, Dr. Price." She paused and her voice changed. "By the way…there haven't been any complaints about *you*."

Involuntarily, Spence's eyes cut to the gray lump filled with unopened letters addressed to him. "I do try." *To avoid desperate women.*

"If you're ever up in Dallas again—"

"I'll give you a call," Spence completed easily, prepared to hang up.

"You do that." Tonya sounded like a woman who'd heard the "I'll call you" line once too often.

"In the meantime, I'll expect some favorable date reports. Nothing terribly detailed—just something to put in our letters column and convince the publisher to hold off on the fraud charges for another month."

The chair squeaked as Spencer sat straight up, eyes wide open. "*Fraud* charges?"

"Yes, an element in our screening procedures— the ones you think need tightening—is the misrepresentation clause in the agreement you and the men in the calendar signed before we agreed to publish your profiles. We rarely have to enforce it, but when we have…" She laughed as though reluctant to reveal the rest. "I'm sure you understand when I tell you it isn't profitable to pursue cases we're likely to lose."

"Cases—you'd take us to court?"

"That's the only method we have for recovering lost revenue and damages to our reputation."

Spencer clicked the monitor back on. The budget glowed into view. "How much revenue are we talking?"

"That's for a jury to decide."

A jury? Being sued would ruin him, even if he won. He'd never receive another grant. And forget staying here. His fund-raising methods—in particular, the calendar—weren't popular with the Research Facility brass. They called them embarrassingly bizarre. Spence called them innovative. The regional press loved him. When they needed a quote, they called Spencer and not the facility chairman, which had become a sore point. Spencer knew the man only tolerated him because his popularity with the press had given the facility a public relations boon.

If *Texas Men* sued, Spencer's project would be shut down. His team, the closest thing he had to a family, would be scattered. At the thought of starting over again, the old familiar queasiness settled in his stomach.

No. Not this time.

"Tonya, I don't think either of us wants to drag what amounts to a difference of opinion into the courts. What, specifically, do you need to reassure your publisher that we've acted in good faith?"

"I told you, written testimonials—"

"Fine. How many?" Spencer grabbed a pencil.

She hedged. "That's difficult to say."

He needed a quantifiable response. "Give me a number."

"Even one is more than I've got now!"

"So I'll get you one."

"Then, Dr. Price, it had better be a heck of a letter."

"Oh, it will be." Even if he had to write it himself.

"We do, of course, subject any correspondence, both positive and negative, to our usual verification procedures."

Nuts. Spencer forced himself to smile. "Of course."

He was still gritting his teeth as he disconnected the call. "Gordon!" he bellowed.

Gordon instantly appeared in the doorway, which meant he'd been listening just outside, a fact Spencer had counted on. What was the good of an open-door policy if no one took advantage of it? Spencer grabbed the message slips and held them up. "You stuck these in the middle of my action file!"

Gordon failed to look repentant. "Somebody should go through his action file more often."

"You're not putting this on me!"

Gordon swallowed and eased his way inside the office. "If you could define 'this' more fully—"

"You yo-yos are about to get us sued!"

As he processed the information, Gordon blinked rapidly, like a malfunctioning android. From past experience, Spencer knew he'd be worthless for the next several minutes.

"Get in here, the rest of you," he called. "And somebody wake up Rip."

"He's not gonna like that," came a voice from outside the door.

"Would you rather have Rip or me angry at you?"

Silence.

They'd obviously failed to grasp the gravity of the situation. Spencer stood, pushed past the blinking Gordon and stepped into the open lab. Without a word to the huddled men, he found the broomstick with the foam pad attached and strode toward the bank of boxes opposite the snack machines.

The six-foot-high stack of boxes formed an L-shape in the rear corner by the rest room and the emergency eye-wash fountain. A blanket had been thumbtacked to the adjacent walls and draped over the top of the boxes. Spencer stood at the entrance to this box cave and blindly shoved the padded end of the broomstick inside until it connected with something.

He poked. Then he poked again. The broomstick stuck.

"This had better be *very* important," sounded a chilling voice from the depths of the darkness.

"Get up, Rip." Spencer was in no mood to play psych games with the brilliant, but socially antagonistic, programmer.

Sebastian "Rip" Riportella preferred to work alone at night in the lab with only the glow from the computer screen and the soft drink vending machine for light.

There was a loud exhaling, then the springs of a cot screeched, reminding Spencer of bats. Rip appeared at the opening between the boxes and the wall. "What crashed?"

"Nothing. We have a public relations glitch."

Rip blinked slowly, his pale gray eyes slightly bloodshot. "You woke me for a glitch?"

"It's a glitch with potential." Spencer pointed to the folding table near the microwave. "Gather round, gentlemen."

Five of them somberly shuffled toward the snack table. Rip dug in the pocket of his black jeans and shoved quarters into the soft drink machine until two cans dropped. He popped one open and sucked it dry before gliding over to join the group.

Spencer wondered if the man existed on anything besides caffeine and sugar. He faced his team. "It appears that the women you've been dating haven't been as enamored of you as you've been of them," he said.

"Is that what this is about?" Dan, a burly programmer, snatched an open bag of nacho-cheese-flavored chips and stuffed a handful into his mouth.

"Yes," Spencer confirmed, and sketched in the details of his conversation with Tonya. "And they're willing to go to court. If that happens, the legal costs will come straight from our research budget." He looked at them squarely. "And that would pretty much be the end of us as a team."

There was silence as everyone avoided eye contact with everyone else.

"Aw, Spence, why didn't you just tell her off?" Dan finished off the bag of chips and wiped his fingers on his T-shirt. "What?" he asked when he saw everyone staring at him.

"Use a paper towel, man." The usually quiet Bob shoved a roll toward him.

"Did—did she actually use the *s* word?" Gordon's blinking was still erratic.

"You mean 'sue'?" Spence asked.

Gordon blinked and nodded.

"No, but she used the *f* word."

"*Did* she?" Rip raised a black eyebrow.

Spencer was in no mood for joking. "Meaning *fraud* in this instance."

"Pity, but still interesting." Rip favored the group with the driest of smiles.

"And expensive, unless she starts getting gushy little notes from the women you guys date. The problem is that the women are expecting one thing and you are another. Now, what's been going on?"

No one wanted to discuss his dating failures in front of everybody, which Spence should have anticipated. He gave them a face-saving out. "I told Tonya that you all have soft hearts and have been dating everybody. Right?"

There were nods all around, except from Rip, who sipped his drink.

"We'll start there." Spencer pulled out a plastic chair and sat so he wouldn't look like he was lecturing, which he was. "Read the letters describing themselves that these women send you and make intelligent choices. That means if a woman mentions her bust size, thinking it's her best attribute, she's going to expect reciprocal attributes from you." He looked significantly at Bob, who ducked his head. "There's not a thing in the world wrong with that, but you don't have either the experience, or the, ah, attributes to handle those kinds of women."

"Well, how are we going to get experience if we don't go out with them?" Gordon had stopped blinking.

"Would you give your 333 MHz Pentium II to a five-year-old to play with? Or would you let him spill his juice on the old 486 until he's ready to up-grade?" Their looks of horror at the thought of a five-year-old with juice near a 333 MHz Pentium II were replaced by murmurs of understanding.

Spencer pointed to the mail sacks. "I want you to cull those letters and find women who say that they don't have a boyfriend because they've been busy getting their masters in computer science, or beta-testing software, or working on the Mars Probe. And show me the letter before you contact her."

"Is that all?" Rip tossed his empty can into the re-cycling bin.

"No. Hand me the calendar."

Dan pulled the one above the microwave off the wall and silently handed it to Spencer.

Wishing December were already at an end so his picture could be covered up by a freebie fractal cal-endar from the Littletree College math department, he flipped through the pages. Except for Spence and Rip, who was Mr. October, everyone had posed for two pictures. "This is going to take serious damage control. Okay, Steve, you've got to wear bulky sweaters with shoulder pads in them. Plan outdoor activities and wear a hat. Goggles, too, if it's appropriate. Dan, hit the gym and get rid of that beer gut."

"It's not a beer gut!"

"A nacho gut, then. And start drinking diet. Murray, grow a goatee."

"No way!"

Spencer pointed to one of his calendar shots. "You gave yourself a goatee in the picture. Grow one. Gordon…" He squinted at the picture, then at Gordon. "Hit the gym, go to a tanning booth and…" Spencer shook his head. "I'm thinking toupee."

The others hooted as Gordon self-consciously fingered his fast-receding hairline. "I'm not wearing a toupee!"

"Glue a baseball cap to your head, then. Bob."

Bob ducked his head as his face reddened.

"Shoulder pads for you, too. Grow your hair out and get contacts."

"Aw, man."

After several seconds of grumbling, everyone fell silent and looked at Rip. He propped a stockinged foot on the chair next to him.

He'd posed at night, shirtless, with a black cape and his shoulder-length hair swirling around him, and a full moon—computer generated—in the background. The chest in the calendar was more robust than the one possessed by the tall, lean—some might say gaunt—man, but that wasn't what worried Spencer. "Rip, have you answered any of the letters?"

A half smile touched the corner of his mouth. "I

dallied with a couple of aspiring nymphs of the night, but they were unworthy."

Spencer hated it when he talked that way. "Make sure anyone you ask out is a night owl like you, got it?"

Rip bowed.

Spence stood. "Everybody hit the mail sacks and remember that I screen before you call."

"What about the budget projections?" Murray asked. "The chem department needs a man-hour estimate."

Spencer had already started for his office. He turned back around. "Don't you get it? There won't be anything left to budget if we have to use all our money to hire lawyers."

"Does that mean you'll be favoring a young lady with your company?" Rip's half smile held a challenge.

"No," Spencer said. "Me dating was never part of the deal."

"And why not?" Holding the calendar, Rip moved forward. "Of all of us, you are the most likely to generate bits of breathless prose to *Texas Men.*"

"You're wrong." He spoke to Rip, but included all of them in his gaze. "I limit my social engagements to women who have no expectations beyond what I'm offering."

Murray snickered. "He's talking *attributes*, guys."

"If you will." Spencer mimicked Rip's bow.

"Rip's right, Doc." Gordon grinned. "Think of what's at stake, here."

Rip dangled the calendar. "'What lucky woman wouldn't like to find Mr. December in her stocking?''' he quoted in his deep voice. "So how about it, Doc?"

Spence glared at them. They were all nodding in agreement with Rip. He might as well concede this point. "One." He held up a finger. "One, and one only." Grumbling to himself, he stalked back to his office and glared at the mail sack.

Well, which lucky woman would it be?

AFTER STUDYING the building roster, Lexi, armed with *Texas Men*, headed for the lab at the end of the hall. There didn't appear to be a receptionist, so Lexi just opened the door and walked in, blinking at the whiteness of it all.

There was a huge open area with workbenches, swing arm lights, thick, black cables snaking over the floor, machines with their electronic entrails exposed, computers and more computers. At the far end was the snack area, littered with fast-food debris, soda cans and coffee mugs, and to the right of that, a mountain of boxes. It was a minute before she realized that human beings were also present.

It appeared that she'd interrupted a meeting. The men had pulled chairs around two of the computer stations where they were intently…going through mail? No one had noticed her. Lexi opened the *Texas Men* magazine.

"Look at this!" One of them suddenly jumped up. "I've got a math teacher!" He kissed a piece of paper before waving it around. "Read it and weep, guys."

"Aw, man."

"Quit gloating, Gordon."

"She got a sister?"

"Why do all women like long walks on the beach?"

Everybody looked at a slight man with thick glasses. "Because that's what you said *you* liked, Bob."

"You told me to!"

"You know better than to listen to everything Steve tells you."

One of them wadded up an envelope and threw it at him. The man with the glasses retaliated.

"Excuse me," Lexi said before the paper fight got out of hand.

At the sound of her voice, all movement stopped and six vaguely familiar-looking men turned to stare at her.

"Could you tell me where I can find..." Lexi stared at the magazine and, avoiding Mr. December for now, picked a name at random, "Gordon Emerson?"

The man who had been waving around the letter pushed aside the guy with the glasses and approached her. "I'm Gordon Emerson."

Lexi blinked, then stared down at the calendar picture of a man waterskiing. A tanned, fit, square-jawed man. She looked up. "I mean *this* Gordon Emerson." She showed him the magazine.

His smile faded. "Guilty."

Acutely aware that she'd just insulted him, Lexi tried to salvage the situation. "Oh, I see now. It's...it's the light in here." Which was very bright. "And—and the goggles, and, uh...you *are?*" Forget salvaging, she had to find the calendar men. On the drive over, she'd convinced herself that nothing less than a Phi Beta Kappa Mr. Universe would stand up to the glory of Emily.

Flipping through the magazine, she walked toward the group as she compared the rest of them to their pictures. There were vague resemblances—enough to tell her she'd come to the right place. "You all are the men from the calendar?"

They nodded, looking irritated and sheepish at the same time.

Okay. They weren't superhuman after all, but they were probably decent guys who might be talked into Christmas dinner. Still, Lexi decided she wouldn't tell Francesca. Let her have her Mr. December fantasies.

"And you are...?"

The rumbling question came from a man she recognized as Mr. October. He sat on the counter next to a soft drink machine and eyed her as he drank from a can. In the photograph, he'd looked dangerously forbidding. Now he just looked dangerous. She mentally crossed him off her list of potential Christmas dates. Besides, Halloween was an element she didn't want to introduce at Christmas.

"I'm Alexandra Jordan. I'm on the faculty at Littletree."

"And how might we be of service?" Mr. October asked.

Lexi hadn't anticipated making her request to all of them at once. "I saw this." She held up the magazine. "And thought I'd skip a couple of steps and come over here."

There was a silence before the man with the glasses spoke. "Y-y-you mean you want to go out with Gordon?"

Lexi remembered his glee at finding the math teacher. "I didn't have any one particular man in mind." *Yes, you did.* "I just..." She trailed off as the meaning of the sacks of mail sank in. This was a bad idea. She should leave while her dignity was still semi-intact. "Sorry to bother you."

"What do you teach, Alexandra?" Mr. October slid off the ledge.

Lexi backed up. "Piano."

He gestured to the group. "Which of you gentlemen can converse on the topic of music?"

"Dan, over there, can play the guitar," Gordon said.

A frowning barrel-shaped man raised his hand.

There was a sneeze. "I played clarinet in the band until my asthma got too bad."

Lexi gazed at them. They were being polite, which was more than she'd been so far. "That's great—not about your asthma. Look, I see that a lot of women responded to your profiles—"

"I know you!" One of the previously silent men got out of his chair and approached her, hand outstretched. "Murray Bendel. I teach chemistry at Littletree."

Not bad. Nothing like his picture, but not bad. Lexi shook his hand, careful to protect her fingers from a crushing grip. Murray's was fine and Lexi relaxed.

"Let me introduce you to Doc," he said.

"Hey—"

Murray sliced a look toward the group. "Doc needs to meet her."

Doc could only mean Spencer Price, Mr. December. Lexi found she didn't want her fantasy destroyed, either. "No, really, that's okay."

But Murray was propelling her toward the only office in the area. "Hey, Doc," he said, pulling her to the doorway. "Meet Alexandra Jordan."

The man had his back to her, his eyes glued to a computer screen. As he swiveled his chair around, he said in a harsh tone, "Murray, I told you to show me the letter before you contacted anyone."

"I didn't write a letter," Lexi said just before she caught sight of his face.

It was Mr. December. In the flesh, or rather not as much flesh as his calendar shot, but she didn't have trouble recognizing him at all because he looked exactly like his photograph. Or better. Yes, better. Much better. No fantasies destroyed here.

The dark eyes in the picture had come to life, looking intelligent even without the photographer's umbrella light reflected in them. And they moved in an up-and-down sweep that made her suck her stomach in.

Before pasting on a polite smile, he glared at Murray behind her, and she recognized the exact expression he'd worn for his photograph.

Involuntarily she looked at the magazine in her hands and turned the page past November to December. Yes, there he was, with his bare torso against a fireplace and a Santa Claus suit slung over his shoulder.

She swallowed and inhaled, unfortunately at the same time.

"You wanted to see me?" he asked when she'd finished coughing.

Ooooh, yes. "Please don't be angry with, uh, Murray." Lexi looked around, but Murray had abandoned her. "He thought I should meet you. I should have called first."

"I never stay angry with men who bring me beautiful women in black leather." He accompanied the flattery with a smile full of perfectly straight, white teeth.

Okay, this man was out of her league, but she'd

known that before. Good grief, he was probably out of Francesca's league. He was out of Francesca's *underwear's* league.

He reached across his desk. "Spencer Price."

Lexi clasped his hand, thinking of the long fingers she'd admired, for once not concerned about possible injury to her own. "Lexi Jordan," she said, though he already knew that.

It was just that once she touched his hand and registered the warmth of it, the rest of the calendar picture came to life and Lexi was rendered speechless. She had absolutely no trouble at all visualizing him without the black T-shirt that advertised a computer chip he was currently wearing.

Spencer sat back in his chair and waited—waited for her to explain why she was there. She couldn't quite form words yet. Actually that wasn't true. The words forming were, *Wanna take a dip in my gene pool?* and Lexi was wishing she hadn't been so hasty in buttoning up that other button.

He was just so incredibly handsome. It was the kind of handsome that takes a few minutes to sink in, and it didn't help to see that he was aware of the effect he had on her.

This was not her finest moment.

"What can I do for you, Ms. Jordan?" he prompted, still polite, but reminding her that time was passing.

Lexi drew a deep breath, wished she had on Francesca's cat suit and blurted out, "Will you come to my family's Christmas dinner?"

3

SPENCER BLINKED. It sounded as though Lexi Jordan had just invited him to Christmas dinner. He scrambled to figure out the connection between them—there must be one. People didn't go around inviting strangers to Christmas dinner.

Before he'd disappeared, Murray had mouthed something behind her and had acted like Spence should know what the heck he meant.

Jordan...Jordan. The name was familiar, but Spence couldn't place it. Was she the daughter or sister of a friend? A donor? They'd never met, of that he was certain. With hair like a black waterfall against that white skin, she was strikingly unforgettable.

Long, silky, shiny hair like hers was a particular weakness of his—and he hadn't known it until just now.

When she'd leaned forward to shake his hand, the ends of her hair had brushed across his wrist, sending more prickles through him than the leftover charge on a power supply capacitor.

"I'm sorry." Smiling at herself, she shook her head, making her hair ripple. "I didn't mean to just blurt it out like that. I should explain."

"Please." Spence gestured to the chair on the other side of his desk.

Lexi looked down at it, but didn't sit. Spencer

stood up, peered over the desk and saw three circuit boards and a spool of solder on the seat. "Just move—I'd better do it." He came from around his desk and picked up the circuit boards, looking helplessly for a flat surface to park them on. Ultimately he dumped them on top of the pile of *Texas Men* mail he'd been sorting through. "There." He smiled and gestured.

She looked dazed, and in the moment before she sat, Spence automatically noted that she was no more than half a foot shorter than he was.

Good, he thought. Any shorter, and certain critical maneuvers during certain activities were a hassle.

Lexi was frowning as she stared at the circuit boards—no, she was staring at the letters under the circuit boards. Spence followed her gaze. Some of the women had sent pictures and he'd put those on top, thinking that they'd already made the first cut, since he wanted to know what his potential date looked like.

A photo of a bare leg that he knew was attached to a real babe of a cellist stuck out from the stack. Lexi tilted her head.

Spence didn't know how much she could see from her angle, so he cleared his throat. "You were going to explain?"

"Oh!" She turned startled eyes toward him. "Oh." She slumped and stared at the magazine in her lap. "I saw the write-up of your research team in *Texas Men,* and since I live in Rocky Falls, I thought that..." Her gaze drifted over to the letters. "It seemed silly to...so I..."

It wasn't much of an explanation, but for the moment Spencer was just enjoying watching her mouth move. She'd put on red lipstick, not the shiny gooey kind, but a frank red, which showed up against her pale skin. He liked the contrast.

A hand-lettered sign appeared in the doorway, drawing his attention away from her lips. It read "Lawrence Jordan." A split second later the top half of Murray's head came into view and his eyebrows wagged.

What were the guys up to now? Spencer kept his face blank. There was a rustling and the faint squeak of a marking pen. A dollar sign joined Lawrence Jordan.

Spencer determinedly jerked his gaze back to Lexi, as his peripheral vision registered more dollar signs and a moving arrow.

The arrow was pointing to her. Dollar signs and Lexi Jordan. Okay. He didn't know the exact connection between Lexi and money, but until he did, he was going to pour on the charm. His smile widened to the point where the dimple in his left cheek would show. He leaned forward, rested his forearms on his desk and toyed with the pens in a coffee mug. Open body language. Relaxed. Approachable.

He watched to see if she'd mimic him, maybe by relaxing her death grip on the magazine. She did, but only to grip the chair instead.

Her lips pursed. "I've never done anything like this before and I guess I don't know the protocol for asking you for a date. Specifically, Christmas dinner at my family's, but I'd like to see you at least once before then, so we'll… Could you please say something?"

And Spencer found himself momentarily at a loss

for words. He should have been paying closer attention. "Why Christmas dinner?"

Lexi's face underwent a subtle transformation from flustered to something else—something harder. She tilted her head. "Why not?"

He kept smiling as he stared at the pen he tapped. "I can think of a hundred reasons why not." He widened his smile as he met her eyes. "I'm interested in why I should."

IF THE DAY HADN'T been dark and rainy, Lexi wouldn't have been able to see the reflection in the window behind Spencer. Backward or not, a dollar sign was easily recognizable.

They'd figured out who she was—or rather, who her father was, and Lexi decided to use that fact to her advantage. Francesca had a naked cello picture, Lexi had a father whose job was to give away money.

The playing field was now level.

Up to this point, Lexi had been having a hard enough time coping with Mr. December in the flesh, what with Francesca's leg staring at her.

The moment she'd seen Spencer Price, she'd known this was a lost cause. This was not the sort of man who liked being pursued by women. *He* liked deciding when, where and *if* he'd make the first move. Lexi didn't know how she knew this, maybe it was something to do with the expression in his calendar photo. But she knew it was true.

She also knew that asking for a date and being turned down was more face-saving than running. Still, until she'd seen the reflection, she'd had to grip the chair bottom to keep from leaping out of it.

Now there was hope, except that she'd been a little premature with the Christmas dinner invitation. She should have started with coffee and worked her way up.

Too late now. She was going to have to run with it—just as soon as she knew where to run. When in doubt, stall. "You want to know why you should come to Christmas dinner."

"Yes." He steepled his hands and looked at her from behind them.

He'd been smiling at her for the past several minutes. Lexi suspected he was trying not to laugh. "For starters," she said, and held up his picture, "you'd get another opportunity to wear your Santa suit. Doesn't look like it got much wear here."

Well, that got rid of the fake smile. In fact, his glare matched the calendar picture.

The signs behind Lexi quivered. In the silence, yet another dollar sign was reflected in the window, and this one had an exclamation point with it.

She should give up and make a deal with him—be her date and meet her father. "The main reason you should come is because the music building is falling apart," she said bluntly.

He dropped his hands. "What?"

"Littletree's music building needs extensive renovations, more practice rooms, new pianos... everything, really. We're losing out on the top student prospects and faculty. My father is chief administrating trustee of the Cultural Arts Foundation." Lexi said that part very distinctly. "I want to approach him on behalf of Littletree, but I want him in a good mood. To be in a good mood, I must bring a..." Lexi searched for the right word. "Date" wasn't exactly it.

"Prospective son-in-law?" Spencer supplied dryly.

That wasn't it, either. Or was it? "Let's say someone my parents would be thrilled to see me involved with." Making Emily hoarse with envy was strictly a bonus. "I was trying to find just the right man when I saw the seven of you in *Texas Men* and decided I'd come over here to meet you."

He didn't say anything. Apparently she needed to spell everything out. "So I need this favor from you, and in return, you'll get to meet my father."

There. At least now if he agreed, he'd know what he'd be getting into and she wouldn't feel guilty for subjecting him to the surreal experience of the Jordan family faking Norman Rockwell.

Spencer sat back in his chair with an expression she couldn't read. "Impeccable logic. I'm impressed."

"I'm also aware that Christmas is a family time, so I understand if you have other plans." Lexi was proud of thinking of an unembarrassing way for him to refuse.

BEHIND HER, Gordon and Murray were mouthing "yes" at him. Spencer had finally figured out who Lawrence Jordan was, but right now, he had a bigger problem than funding, and an attractive solution had just walked into his office, saving him untold amounts of time and energy. Now he could quit going through the mail and get back to the budget. What a thrill.

"We're a Christmas Eve family, and my parents

live in Dallas." Foster parents, but he didn't think the distinction would matter. "So Christmas afternoon is doable." He gestured, hoping the guys would take the hint and leave. They didn't.

"You mean you'll come?" Hope lit her eyes.

He hadn't noticed her eyes before. They were kind of lost next to her hair and lips, but they were nice eyes. Blue when he'd expected brown. "There are certain conditions," he said.

The sparkle faded. "There always are."

He ignored that. "If I agree to play adoring boyfriend for you, I'll need a return favor." He opened and shut drawers, looking for paper. Finding a blank sheet without the lab logo, he cleared a space on his desk and pushed the paper in front of her, along with a pen he'd taken from the coffee mug. "I want you to write *Texas Men* and tell them..." Tell them what? "Let me see that," he said, gesturing to the magazine in her lap.

Lexi handed it over.

Spencer looked for the letters column and read a couple of the notes. "Tell them what a wonderful time you had on our date, what a great guy I am, how glad you are that you called *Texas Men*—uh, better call them first so you can get into their computer."

"At two ninety-five a minute?"

"Here—use the lab phone." He turned it to face her, then jerked it back. "Wait, they probably keep track of the numbers and it'll look suspicious if the lab's shows up. Here, I'll pay you back." He stood and reached into the back pocket of his jeans.

"Keep it. I'm sure you're worth two ninety-five a minute."

He grinned. "Thanks. I think." Gesturing to the paper, he said, "Start writing. I want to read it before you mail it to them."

"Excuse me…Christmas isn't for another three weeks. Won't they find it a tiny bit strange that I'm raving about something that hasn't happened yet?"

Did he have to think of everything himself? "Don't write about Christmas. Tell them I took you out for pizza and a movie."

"How lame." Lexi sat back in the chair. "Nobody wants to read about pizza and a movie. They want to hear about a romantic date."

Right. As a rich man's kid, she'd never had to think twice about the expense of pizza and a movie. "So, what does that mean? The Wainright Inn?"

"After paying two ninety-five a minute to get your address, it better."

"Why do you like that overpriced place?"

"It's got atmosphere."

Spencer rolled his eyes. "Atmosphere means they put in forty-watt bulbs, light a couple of candles and double the menu prices. Or triple them, if they've got some second-rate musical entertainment sleepwalking their way through Broadway's top tunes."

Her eyes turned glacial.

"Oh, don't tell me, it's got *memories* for you, right? Figures. It's the most expensive place in town."

She sat straight in the chair. "My roommate and I perform there three nights a week. And we do not sleepwalk through anything."

He winced.

A muffled groan sounded from outside his office door. Great. The guys must be eavesdropping, hoping to pick up dating pointers.

Giving her a rueful look, he said, "You probably shouldn't mention this conversation in the letter."

She looked off into the distance. "I can't write the letter. I feel strangely uninspired."

Spencer drew a long breath, then reached into the mail sack and dumped an armful of envelopes onto his desk. "You see this? If you won't write *Texas Men*, then I'm going through this bunch until I find a woman who will." He gave her a smug smile. "And I don't think it'll be too difficult." Just for added emphasis, he picked up an envelope and slowly tore it open.

Lexi leaned an elbow on his desk. "Think of all the time it will take to charm somebody by taking her out for pizza and a movie. Especially when she lives in…"

Before he realized what she was doing, Lexi had plucked the envelope from his fingers and checked the return address.

"El Paso." With a smile equal in smugness to the one he'd just given her, she tossed the envelope back to him.

And he tossed her words back to her. "Think of all the time it will take to find somebody to impress your parents at Christmas dinner."

Her smile slipped. "No time at all. My father *is* Lawrence Jordan. I'll buy a date if nothing else."

And Spencer realized that was exactly what she was doing right now. Dinner in exchange for meeting her father.

He didn't like the idea of being bought.

She stared at him. The flat expression in her eyes made him increasingly uncomfortable. To her, there was no future between them other than this business deal, and that bothered Spencer. Even in business deals, he liked the undercurrent that ran between two people who found each other attractive. It wasn't always appropriate to act upon that attraction, but harmless flirting kept things from being boring.

Lexi Jordan wasn't a woman who was bowled over by good looks—and he'd been trying. Other than being flustered at first meeting him, she'd given no sign that she'd found him irresistibly appealing. She might be hiding her reaction, but Spencer wasn't sure. And that was a new experience for him. He got the impression that it would take a lot to win her over. Might be interesting to try.

He exhaled. To encounter both Lexi and Tonya in one day was more than a man's ego should have to bear.

He primed himself to be conciliatory. "Look. We both know we can solve our problems elsewhere, but we can save time by working together right now. How about it?"

She eyed him. "You must really need this letter."

Spencer scanned the top of the pile, searching for any postmark within fifty miles. None. Several letters were from out of state. "Yes," he admitted.

"If I write the letter now, how do I know you'll show up on Christmas?"

So now he had to put up with insults, too? "Because I said I will! And let me tell you, I didn't grow up with money. There was a time in my life when all I had was my word. You can take it to the bank—because it's guaranteed one hundred percent."

Lexi flinched when Spencer said the word *money.* She'd grown up with the foundation money, all right, but it wasn't hers. It wasn't her father's, either. He was the foundation funds administrator, but the Jordans hadn't set up the foundation. People forgot the distinction, and her parents—especially her mother—didn't go out of their way to correct them. The Jordans moved in the social circles of the foundation's wealthy donors, but as far as Lexi knew, they were merely "comfortable."

She decided not to correct Spencer's assumptions. He wanted to meet Lawrence Jordan, so fine, she'd introduce him to her father—for all the good it would do him. The Cultural Arts Foundation didn't fund scientific projects.

"Okay," she said simply. Tilting the paper toward her, she started writing the date.

"Date it a couple of days from now," Spencer instructed. "Wait. What's today—Wednesday? Okay, say you call and mail your letter today." He bounced a pencil as he thought. "Give it a couple of days to get to me and for me to call you. We go out this weekend.... Date it Sunday, or Monday."

Lexi glanced up at him before doing so. "You realize that I want more than just a warm body to show up for dinner."

Nodding to the paper, Spencer said, "The more enthusiastic you make your letter, the more enthusiastic I'll be."

"It might take more than enthusiasm," she warned, wondering how much of the actual dinner situation she should reveal.

He gave her a heavy-lidded look that shouldn't be seen outside the bedroom, and spoke in a low, husky voice. "I'll be ready for whatever you need."

Nodding, she said, "That's a good expression, and the fact that you can fake it on command might come in handy. Yeah. This could work." She smiled at him.

Spencer looked like he'd caught a surprise punch in the stomach. What? He didn't expect her to take him seriously, did he?

"By the way, does the name Emily DeSalvo mean anything to you?"

He shook his head. "Should it?"

"Only if you like opera."

"Not particularly."

"Great. Okay, let's see. 'Dear *Texas Men*'" she said as she wrote. "'I decided to give myself an early Christmas present by calling one of the men in your magazine. I chose Mr. December, Spencer Price, because he looked like he could use some Christmas cheer.'"

"Hey!"

"Well, look at your picture," Lexi countered. "You're glaring."

"Not on purpose," he said with an appealing defensiveness. "The photographer was being a jerk. All this 'pump up and give me sexy' talk. And I was not going to put on that stupid suit."

Lexi studied the picture. "Oh, I agree. You were right not to put on the suit."

Spencer cleared his throat. "The letter?"

She looked at what she'd written. "'But when he called me, he was as nice as—'"

"Not *nice*," Spencer interrupted. "You don't call a guy nice unless he's somebody's brother or cousin or something."

Lexi crossed out *nice*. "I'm assuming this is a rough draft?"

"It is now."

"'—he was as charming—'"

"No. Say something like 'a stud beyond my wildest dreams.'"

He looked serious. When she didn't write, he glanced up at her. "What?"

"I can have some pretty wild dreams. I think I'll change that sentence to 'we clicked right away.'" She raised her eyebrows for confirmation.

"Yeah, okay."

"'He took me to…'"

"Shoot pool at Busters."

"'A faculty concert at Littletree.'" She looked up at him. He rolled his eyes. "The concerts are usually free," she told him.

"Oh, well, then. By all means. And afterwards I sprang for coffee cake at KK's."

"'Afterward, we had white chocolate raspberry truffle cheesecake at the Wainright Inn.'"

His disgusted expression made her laugh.

"What is with you and that place?"

"The faculty concert was free, so quit complaining. 'We talked for hours.'"

"I told you all about the project here, right? We're in beta development for a robotic hand that has tactile—"

"'He wanted to know all about me. At some point, I must have told him my favorite flower, because the next morning, he knocked on my door and brought me coffee, a croissant and a single peach rose—'"

"Peach? No, babe. You were made for red roses."

"But they're such a cliché."

Spencer eyed her. "Black hair, white skin, red

lips...nah. You're a red rose girl. The deep, bloodred kind."

They stared at each other. These offhand comments stirred Lexi in a way his fake sensuality never could. "Roses are okay, but I actually like bright wildflowers. I thought the peach rose would sound better for the letter."

"Good thinking. Can you put in there that we came here for a tour of the lab and you met the other guys and thought they were real studs, too?"

Lexi winced. The men were probably right outside the door, listening. Yes, that last sneeze sounded close by. "'We spent that day together, too—'"

"Come on, I've got to work sometime."

"It's Sunday."

"Oh."

"'Spencer took me on a tour of his lab. I met the other men who appeared in your magazine and they were very friendly.'" She looked at the window behind Spencer. There wasn't anything reflected there, but she could sense that the men weren't far away. "'It was overwhelming to see them all at once. Their work is fascinating.'"

"Cutting edge."

Lexi sighed. "Crossing out 'fascinating,' inserting 'cutting-edge.' 'Anyway, I just wanted you to know how happy I am that I was able to meet Spencer through your magazine. He'll be coming to Christmas dinner at my house—'"

Spencer laughed.

"'...so I know I'll have a Merry Christmas. I hope you have one, too.' How's that?"

"Not bad," Spencer said. "You could say that

you're gaga over me, or I'm everything you expected and more."

"I've only known you two days."

"But I brought you a rose. I fed you cheesecake."

"You took me to shoot pool and fed me stale chips out of the vending machine in the lab."

"The chips aren't in the machine long enough to get stale."

She thought of the wrappings littering the snack bar area and silently agreed with him. "But is the letter to your specifications?"

"You tell me. Is it the kind of letter that would make women want to contact us?"

Lexi looked pointedly at the mail sack. "You *want* more letters?"

"No! To tell you the truth, I didn't want any letters." He rubbed his forehead. "I...haven't answered any of them, and, well, now that I've got your report on our date, I won't have to."

"Do you already have a girlfriend?" Wouldn't that put a crimp in her plans.

"No."

"But if you didn't want to date anyone, then why were you in *Texas Men?*"

He waved his arm. "The others wanted to, and I was part of the calendar."

The best part, Lexi thought. "Okay. Let me recopy this and—ohmigosh, I've got a class in less than ten minutes!"

She scooped up the letter, shoved it inside the magazine and looped her purse over her shoulder. "I've got to run."

This close to finals, she couldn't afford to let a class walk. She started for the door.

"Wait!" Spencer came after her.

"Don't worry. I'll call the magazine." Lexi ran out the door, her purse swinging wide and catching one of the listening men in the stomach. "Sorry."

"The letter—"

"I'll recopy it." She grabbed her purse.

"But I want to read it before you mail it."

Lexi jerked open the lab door. "I'll be in touch."

"But—"

She didn't wait to hear the rest as the door closed behind her.

"But I don't know your phone number," Spencer yelled at the closing door.

He expected her to stick her head back in the door and tell him her number. His mind was ready to receive and process the information. Women gave him phone numbers all the time and he had a good memory for them.

He waited, but all he heard were her footsteps running down the hallway.

And the agitated murmur growing behind him.

"Well, I'm impressed," Rip said.

The only thing worse than knowing Lexi Jordan had left holding the upper hand was knowing that he had to turn around, face his team and pretend that things were exactly the way he wanted them.

He turned and hooked a thumb over his shoulder. "She has a class."

"We heard." Murray wheeled a chair in front of his computer.

"Then you also heard that she's going to write a letter to *Texas Men.*" Spence smiled his best pep-talk smile. "That'll get us off the hook for now, but for in-

surance, you should still try to impress your dates."
He headed for his office.

"The way you impressed her?" Gordon asked,
stopping Spence in his tracks.

He swung his arm and spun on his heel. "There
was a lot going on, body language-wise, that you
couldn't see."

"And aren't you glad?" Dan's snickers were echoed by the others.

"What is this?" Spence asked. "Goals were met
here. We needed a letter. We've got a letter. This was
a successful encounter."

Rip gave him a dark look and dug in his pocket
for quarters. On his way to the soft drink machine,
he asked, "And where is this letter?"

"With her, so she can recopy it."

Everybody exchanged looks.

"Hey, guys, knock it off," Murray said from his
computer. "This is Lexi Jordan we're talking about
here. Her old man is loaded. He runs a foundation
or something. I'll have the specs pulled up in a minute. But Doc knows what he's doing. He doesn't
want to scare her off. She probably has guys hitting
on her all the time, but Doc's too smart for that. So
he's acting like Mr. I-Don't-Care. Puts her off balance, you know?"

"Is that right?" Bob asked.

All eyes were on Spencer. He smiled and clapped
his hands. "Murray, I couldn't have said it better
myself."

4

"WHITE COTTON RULES!" Lexi yelled as soon as she opened the front door. Belatedly, she wondered if all Francesca's students had left for the day. If they hadn't, Francesca would have to explain Lexi's comment, and her underwear preferences would become common knowledge among the Littletree music students.

"What happened?" Francesca was in the kitchen, apparently alone with the cheesecake.

Francesca was not to be trusted with cheesecake.

"I have a date for Christmas dinner!"

She heard a scream. "With one of the calendar cuties? No way!"

Lexi quickly hung up Francesca's coat and arrived in the kitchen in time to catch her roommate shoving a plastic container back into the refrigerator.

"Aw, Frankie, you've been eating the cheesecake. You know we hardly ever get cheesecake leftovers."

Francesca swallowed. "And we wouldn't have this time, but the flaming brandied mincemeat cheesecake wasn't a popular flavor. I don't know why not. It's great after you scrape off the mincemeat."

"Will I get a chance to taste it for myself?"

"If you're fast." Licking the fork, Francesca tossed it into the sink. "Now what happened? Did you have trouble finding the men? Are they gorgeous? Who's your date with? Tell me everything."

Lexi grinned. "I showed my faculty ID to the guard and he waved me through. Then I went into the building, looked them up in the directory—they all work together—and just walked into the lab."

"Just like that?"

Lexi nodded.

"No—no hordes of women clawing at their clothes?"

Laughing, Lexi shook her head. "They should be glad I'm not a terrorist."

Francesca could hardly contain herself. "I may pay a visit to the lab, myself. So…who is it?"

Lexi hesitated, then blurted out, "Mr. December!"

There was silence as Francesca stared at her in stunned disbelief.

Lexi knew just how she felt.

"Not Mr. December."

"Mr. December."

"*My* Mr. December?"

"Well, Francesca…"

"I need more cheesecake." She jerked open the refrigerator door. "Did you ask him if he got my picture?"

Lexi thought of the naked leg. "No, I didn't ask."

Carrying the cheesecake, Francesca walked past her. She parked herself next to the silverware drawer and got out a fork. "Let me get this straight…. You just *walked* into the lab and asked this guy to come to Christmas dinner. And he agreed?"

It would be hugely gratifying to pretend that she'd instantly captivated the most gorgeous man in Rocky Falls, if not the entire state of Texas, but she had to live with Francesca—and she wanted some of that cheesecake. "He agreed because he wants to meet my father."

Frankie paused, the fork halfway to her mouth. "He told you that?"

Lexi remembered seeing the signs reflected behind her. "He didn't have to. It was obvious."

"That stinks." Francesca offered her a fork.

"But I can work with it." Lexi took the fork and managed three bites of okay-tasting cheesecake. She surrendered the rest to her roommate. "I mean, Francesca, this guy is incredible."

"Well, I knew that."

"So does he. But I didn't mind, because if he didn't know it, then he'd be stupid and not worth the trouble." She looked off into space. "He's got this shallow dimple on one side...." Lexi pressed her own cheek. "It only shows when he gets this look in his eyes and smiles a certain way."

"All right, don't rub it in," Francesca grumbled. "Oh, I forgot. Gwen called and wants to know if we can fill in for her at the Wainright tonight."

"Tonight?" Lexi didn't want to go out tonight. She wanted to stay in and memorize Spencer Price's write-up in *Texas Men*. "Did she get a better-paying gig?"

"Yeah. She's been booked for Britten's 'A Ceremony of Carols' and the choir rehearsal is tonight."

Lexi wasn't surprised. "Harpists can really pull in major cash this time of year."

Francesca finished the last of the cheesecake. "If we take her place tonight we can, too. Plus, think of the leftovers. And by the way, you can have the prime rib. I like mine rare, and microwaving overcooks it."

Leftovers from the Wainright Inn's kitchen heavily supplemented Lexi and Francesca's food budget. However... "My parents will be there tonight. There's some fund-raiser in the wine cellar."

Lawrence and Catherine Jordan had made no secret of the fact that they felt Lexi was wasting her talent by playing dinner music at the Wainright Inn, even though it boasted a highly acclaimed regional theater and had been named one of the Southwest's top ten undiscovered treasures. Lexi liked to think that meant she was a treasure, too.

But Emily would never stoop to providing dinner music, they said.

Well, bully for Emily. When the Met called Lexi, she'd quit playing dinner music.

"Lexi, please?" Francesca had on her I've-found-new-underwear-I-want-to-buy look.

"Oh, all right. But let's leave our publicity poster in the storeroom." There was a chance Lexi's parents wouldn't notice she was there unless they deliberately walked through the main dining room.

"Sure." Francesca eyed her. "You know, I ran across some Egyptian cotton underwear with lace cutwork panels. I didn't order it, but now I'm thinking of giving cotton a try, since you've had such good luck with it."

Lexi laughed. "Just for that, tonight I'll wear black undies."

AN HOUR AFTER Lexi had left, Spencer knew as much about her as it was possible to know from computer data bases. And since the lab was networked into the Littletree main computer, he knew a lot.

For instance, he knew her class rosters, what she taught, the grades she'd given the previous semester, her schedule, her address and phone number, her driver's license and social security numbers. He'd read her résumé, and knew that the campus clinic had given her Benadryl for a cold in November.

Littletree ought to restrict access to those files, Spencer thought, as he ran a search on her father. But as long as they hadn't, he felt no compunction about learning as much as he could.

He gave a low whistle. Murray had been right. Lawrence Jordan's foundation had given away hundreds of thousands of dollars, mostly to museums, schools and performing groups, both in Rocky Falls, Austin and other arts communities in the area. No scientific grants, but that didn't mean Spencer's project couldn't be the first. Money was money.

He smiled. If there was one thing he knew how to do, it was go after money. "Hey, Murray," he called from his office. "Thanks for the heads-up about Lexi's father."

"No prob." Murray and the others had gone back to work. Rip had disappeared into his cave.

Spencer was torn. On one hand, he wanted his staff to work, but on the other, he wanted more than one glowing letter winging its way to *Texas Men,* for their morale, if nothing else.

And *his* letter wasn't a certainty. Lexi Jordan had run out of the lab before Spencer could close the deal the way he liked. Matters were unfinished between them. Yes, she said she'd call him. No, he didn't like fitting himself to her timetable. He wanted to verify that she'd called *Texas Men* and recopied the letter.

Staring at the printout of information he'd gleaned, he found her phone number and called her house.

The voice on the answering machine wasn't hers. He called again, got the same voice and hung up. Spencer Price didn't do messages.

Where was she? It was around dinnertime, so she could have gone out...except she played at the Wainright Inn several nights a week.

Spencer called the Wainright Inn. "Who's your musical entertainment tonight?" he asked the woman who answered the phone.

"Tonight, Francesca Fontaine and Alexandra Jordan will be performing. Cello and piano."

Okay, her turf it was. Spencer made a reservation.

He walked out of his office to find five pairs of eyes watching him. "I'm going to go hear her play," he explained. "What's the big deal?"

A chorus of "Nothing" answered him. They all went back to what they'd been doing. Spencer hoped they were paying attention. He was taking immediate steps to pursue Lexi Jordan. He wasn't waiting around; he was seizing the moment.

The moment just happened to be at the Wainright Inn.

"Gordon, will you lock up tonight?" he asked.

"Sure."

"In that case, gentlemen, I'm off to put on my money suit."

"LET'S NOT PLAY *Cats* tonight," Lexi said. She and Francesca had taken their places and she was sounding a series of "A's" on the piano while Francesca tuned her cello.

"Please? I need a break and I can play 'Memory' in my sleep."

Spencer's comment about the talent at the Wainright Inn was too fresh in Lexi's mind for her to let that pass. "Oh, go take off your underwear and put a little extra into your playing."

Francesca adjusted a peg. "And what's with you? Did somebody's cotton shrink in the drier?"

Lexi looked out over the dining room. It was the first seating on a Wednesday night, but the place was packed. The Wainright Inn had a great reputation, and many people drove from Texas's larger cities to eat in the quiet elegance. "I just think we owe it to these people to give our best performance."

"I very much hope you aren't implying anything about the quality of my playing." Francesca's eyes looked like they were capable of shooting fire.

"I don't want us to get stale, okay?"

Francesca tossed her head and signaled that she was ready to begin.

Lexi glanced at Francesca's music stand and saw the *Broadway's Top Forty* book open. Deliberately she opened *Going for Baroque*, and began playing the introduction.

Francesca made a strangled sound, then slowly closed her book and got out the Baroque one. She quietly checked her tuning, which Lexi knew was perfectly in pitch, tightened her bow, tested it, then loosened it.

In the meantime, Lexi had finished the introduction, and was forced to noodle around—hoping that nobody seated in the dining room was a Baroque scholar—before beginning again.

This time Francesca began playing when she was supposed to.

But Francesca had been known to hold a grudge, and Lexi knew all was still not forgiven when they began their fourth selection, a gigue. The lively dance had Lexi playing triplets against Francesca's single-note bass line.

Francesca played first and she set a tempo that was going to have Lexi scrambling to keep up.

"Slow down, Frankie, it's not a horse race," Lexi hissed.

"I don't want us to get stale," Francesca said smugly.

All right. Fine. The piece became a tug-of-war as Lexi's fingers flew over the keys. She was determined to make it all the way through without tangling her fingers, and Francesca was just as determined to keep the tempo fast.

They ended in a flourish that had Lexi out of breath.

A smattering of applause rippled across the room. It was rare that people interrupted their eating to notice the music, and it probably meant their musical tug-of-war had been observed, but Lexi and Francesca stood to bow, anyway.

"*That* was unprofessional," Lexi said through her smile.

"*That* was exhilarating." Francesca took an extra bow, though she didn't deserve to. "We should play it that way every night."

"Then you'll play it alone."

They took their seats.

"Oh, look. It's the Handel." Francesca positioned her bow. "Lots of lovely sixteenth notes, Lexi."

Lexi stared at a piece that was worse than the gigue.

"Unless you think everyone is ready for a change of pace?"

Lexi glared at her, then took out the *Broadway's Top Forty* book and banged out the introduction to the *Cats* medley.

"Tsk, tsk," Francesca whispered. "We owe it to our audience to give our best performance."

Which is how Lexi came to be playing Broadway show tunes after all when Spencer Price walked into the dining room. Alone.

Francesca hadn't noticed him yet because she was overemoting as she played "Memory," but Lexi had been looking around the room to see if she knew any of the diners.

As soon as she saw Spencer, she stared at her music, even though she had it memorized. What was he doing here? He hated this place.

She stole a look at him as he was being seated at a table right in the middle of the room. By swiveling her eyes, she could see him without turning her head.

He was dressed in a dark suit and white collarless shirt, and his hair was slicked back. If she hadn't known better, she'd think her parents had had him made to order.

He was perfect. No, he redefined perfection. He set new standards for the male gender. He—

"What are you doing?"

Lexi jerked her eyes back to Francesca. They hurt from staring to the side. "Playing."

"We just finished 'Memory'!"

Lexi focused on the music. Apparently she'd repeated one too many times. "This is an encore."

Francesca started playing again, but softer. "What is the matter with you?"

"So I got distracted. Don't tell me it's never happened to you."

"It's never happened to me."

"Oh, really?" Lexi stared at Francesca's self-righteous profile. "Mr. December is sitting at table fourteen."

Francesca's bow jerked. "Omigawd." She stared.

"And just think—maybe he's seen you naked," Lexi added evilly.

Francesca mangled the last notes. Lexi played louder, since Francesca's performance had deteriorated.

"Omigawd," she said again. "I'm sweating. We're breaking after *Fiddler on the Roof*."

They weren't due to finish the set for another fifteen minutes, but Lexi wasn't about to argue.

The last notes of "Sunrise, Sunset" had barely faded away before she and Francesca had hopped off the platform and were slipping out to the anteroom.

As soon as the door closed behind them, Francesca rounded on her. "How could you ask him to come here tonight without telling me?"

"I didn't!"

"Then why is he here?"

"Dinner?" But Lexi knew he must be here to see her, since no one had come to join him.

"Lexi, did you see him?" Francesca's eyes looked glazed.

"Yes. I'm the one who pointed him out."

"No, I mean did you *see* him. Isn't he gorgeous? Omigawd."

Very eloquent, Lexi thought.

"I can't believe you actually asked him out. I would have choked on my drool."

Before Lexi succumbed to a retroactive attack of nerves, there was a knock and Julian Wainright, the owner, looked in. "Alexandra, the gentleman at table fourteen has invited you to join him."

Francesca squealed and grabbed her arm.

Julian sent her an amused glance. "Are you interested? I can vouch for him. His name is Spencer Price and he's a head honcho over at the Electronics Research Facility. Excellent taste in wine, as well. The waitstaff tells me he's a generous tipper when it's warranted."

"We've met." Lexi peeled Francesca's fingers off her arm.

"What shall I tell him?"

Francesca poked her.

"Tell him I'll be right out."

"And that I'm coming with her."

Julian nodded and left.

Lexi took a step forward, only to be jerked back by Francesca. "What are you doing?"

"Don't go rushing out there. Make him wait a little. Anticipation heightens the pleasure."

Lexi rolled her eyes. "I'm not playing games. We don't have a relationship like that." She pushed open the door.

"You have a *relationship?*"

Lexi ignored her and concentrated on walking between the tables without catching her long skirt on anything.

Spencer stood at their approach. His smile made her knees wobble a bit, but other than that, Lexi negotiated the tables without incident.

"I'll bet you didn't expect to see me here," he said, holding a chair for her.

"Knowing this isn't your favorite dining spot in Rocky Falls, no."

"But it's *your* favorite, so I thought I'd give it another chance." He flashed his smile at her—the one with the dimple.

Behind her, Francesca whimpered. Or it could have been her underwear whimpering.

Lexi reached behind her and dragged Frankie to the side so Spencer wouldn't think *she'd* made the sound. "This is my music partner and roommate, Francesca Fontaine."

It was gratifying for Lexi to see that the woman who'd sent a naked picture of herself with her cello, the same woman who conversed with his picture every morning, was also reduced to speechlessness when face-to-face with Spencer Price.

As they shook hands, Spencer cocked his head. "Have we met before?"

"Oh, I would have remembered," Frankie gushed.

Lexi knew the exact moment when it occurred to her roommate why she might look familiar. Her eyes widened, then narrowed in self-satisfaction. "Though if you think about it, I'm sure the reason I look familiar will come to you."

Okay, that was enough. They were all still standing in the center of the room and there were only two chairs at the table. Lexi was sending telepathic messages to her oblivious roommate, urging her to leave when Spencer spoke.

"I'll do that," he said. "In the meantime, I don't want to take up your break while Lexi and I discuss a mutual project."

Even Francesca couldn't ignore that. She sent him a sizzling look, then sashayed back to the anteroom. Lexi adjusted her chair so she blocked her brazen roommate's retreat.

"Do you have a few minutes to talk?" Spencer asked her.

"Sure," Lexi said, determined to present a casual contrast to Francesca, since there was no way she could compete with her.

"Have you eaten? Or would you care for a glass of wine?"

"Ordinarily I'd gladly accept. But tonight I've got another ninety minutes of performing to get through. Tomato juice would be fine, though."

All Spencer had to do was glance over his shoulder and a waitress appeared. The female contingent was obviously keeping their eyes on him.

Lexi didn't blame them at all.

After ordering her tomato juice, Spencer leaned forward on his elbows and the votive candle in the center of the table cast shadows under his eyebrows and cheekbones. Lexi shivered.

"Did you remember to call *Texas Men?*" he asked, his voice low and seductive—or at least that's the way it sounded to Lexi.

Unfortunately she hadn't called. "I didn't get home until after five, and that's when I learned

Frankie and I were scheduled to play here tonight. This isn't our regular night."

"So you haven't called *Texas Men*."

Boy, he knew how to make a person feel guilty. "No, but I will. I said I would."

"Good, because I'm going to bug you until you do."

Having him leave her alone was supposed to motivate her to call?

"And don't forget the letter."

She'd forgotten the letter. "I'm researching as we speak."

"Then I'd better start speaking about something else." He gestured to the piano with his eyes. "You play very well."

He'd unknowingly summed up her musical career. "Very well" wasn't great, or fabulous, or stupendous, or transcendent, or sublime, or magical— all words used to describe Emily's singing. But she wouldn't tell him.

"Thanks. We like show tunes," she added, wishing he could have arrived during their gigue duel.

He gave her a charmingly rueful grin that looked so attractive, Lexi wondered if he'd practiced it in front of a mirror. "Still haven't forgiven me for that crack, have you?"

"I was unaware that you wanted to be forgiven."

SPENCER BLINKED then sat back and crossed his arms as he studied her. He was getting nowhere with her.

Did ice water run in her blue-blooded veins?

Or had she somehow figured out his wrong-side-of-the-tracks background?

No. He wasn't going to think that way. The prejudice he'd endured growing up was an old wound that had healed long ago. He chose to ignore the occasional painful twinge. "You don't like me much, do you?" Sometimes the direct approach was best.

A flush tinged her pale skin. "I don't know you."

Spencer relaxed. She was reserved; that was it. He found her reserve refreshing. And surprising, considering the hot little number she had as a roommate. "We'll have to remedy that."

"Yes, we will," she said with a frank smile, and sipped her tomato juice. "But I don't think ten minutes now will get us through Christmas dinner."

He hadn't been thinking about Christmas dinner. He'd been thinking about her, and the way she'd looked when he'd first seen her at the piano. He wondered if she knew how she looked when she played. She put her whole body into her music, bringing new life into the worn-out melodies she was playing.

And her face... He could hardly believe the woman coolly regarding him across the table was the same woman whose face so transparently expressed the emotions of the music she was playing.

Or maybe she *was* expressing her emotions. Maybe she wasn't interested. Maybe she... Wait a minute. In his mind, Spencer replayed her last remark, something about ten minutes not being long enough.

An opening, and he'd missed it. Was he *that* out of practice? "We'll have to get together," he said, hoping she hadn't noticed the gap. "We could have dinner here some night when you aren't performing. What's a good day for you?"

And for some reason he couldn't fathom, she

smiled, and her smile kept getting wider until it lit up her whole face.

He blinked at the transformation and wondered if good old Julian offered frequent eater cards. Because if bringing her to this place made her smile like that, then that's what Spencer was going to do.

"What a sweetie!"

"Me?" No one called him "sweetie." "Sweetie" didn't fit his image.

She nodded and tucked her hair behind her ear. "You're willing to come back here with me because you know I like it, when we could just as easily talk in either of our offices or on the phone."

Spencer wouldn't mind doing more than talking, but he figured now wasn't the time to mention it. This was the first breakthrough he'd had with her.

"You know what, though?"

Spencer shook his head.

"I think I'd like you to teach me to shoot pool at Busters."

An image of Lexi bending over a pool table in a tight skirt about as long as her hair flashed into his mind. "Okay." He grinned. "Okay."

Oookay.

Lexi pushed up the sleeve of her turtleneck and looked at her watch. "We should start again in five minutes. Francesca is going to ask me questions about you and I haven't got anything more to tell her, except that I'm going to learn to shoot pool."

Francesca, her partner. Spencer was having trouble remembering what she looked like. "What do you want to know?"

"For starters, tell me what's true and what's not true in your *Texas Men* write-up."

"The education stuff is right because that's all I'd give them. They had to make up everything else."

She seemed disappointed. "So you aren't looking for a woman to help you finish building your mountain cabin where you'd spend long winter nights making love by the fire?"

He felt like he'd had the wind knocked out of him. "I don't have a mountain cabin." But it was sounding like a darn good idea. "And do you see any mountains around here?"

"They didn't say where it was."

Spencer drew a deep breath to make sure he still could.

"I suppose I should have read the thing."

"You didn't even read it?"

"Not much point. Basically, on good days, I work on the robotic hand we're developing. On other days, I have to raise money to fund the project."

"And that's what the calendar was."

Spencer nodded. "Worked great, too. So—give me a quick sound bite about you."

And her face changed again—it sort of closed up.

What had he said?

"You're going to get more than a sound bite." Her voice was strained as she stared over his shoulder. "You're going to get to meet my parents."

5

HERE? NOW? Though Spencer had on his money suit, he wasn't yet prepared to make his first impression on Lawrence Jordan. He hadn't studied the man. Hell, he was barely acquainted with the daughter.

Of all the rotten luck.

Apparently his sentiments were echoed by Lexi. With a wary smile, she continued to gaze over his shoulder. The fingers gripping the tomato juice were white at the tips. Great. Tense family relations. His favorite.

"Hey...how friendly are we?"

"It depends. Moderately, I suppose."

"Then look at me and smile."

She made the effort, but without any success. He crossed his eyes and was rewarded with a surprised laugh. She relaxed marginally, then stared at her parents again. Spencer judged the Jordans' progress across the dining room by Lexi's ever-tightening grip on her glass.

Right. Standing, he turned to find an attractive older couple approaching them. They were tall, thin and well dressed. Spencer had met their kind a hundred times before. He wished he could reassure her.

Lexi's parents were regarding him with undisguised curiosity, sizing him up, reserving judgment.

He heard the scrape of Lexi's chair as she stood, too.

"Alexandra, I didn't expect to see you this evening. You're working, I take it." Her mother advanced with outstretched hands. She clasped Lexi's and they exchanged an air kiss before Mrs. Jordan faced him, obviously waiting for an introduction.

Lexi obliged. "Mom, Dad, this is Dr. Spencer Price. Spencer, these are my parents."

Dragged up the social ladder by his title, but that was okay by him. Whatever worked. "Delighted to meet you, Mr. and Mrs. Jordan." Spencer shook Lawrence's hand in his best pressing-the-flesh style. "Would you care to join us?" Spencer was fairly certain they'd decline. At least he hoped so. With Lexi's break nearly over, an acceptance meant he'd be alone with them.

"Thank you, but no. We're attending a function in the wine cellar and just stopped by to say hello," Mrs. Jordan said. Then she added, "Did Alexandra introduce you as *Dr.* Price?"

"Yes, I head up a team at the research facility."

"*Do* you?" Mrs. Jordan thawed considerably, bestowing a look of surprised approval on her daughter.

It made Spence wonder about the kind of men Lexi normally hung out with.

"And what sort of things do you research?" Mrs. Jordan asked.

If Lexi had been having an easy time of it, Spence would have limited his remarks to social nothings. But Lexi wasn't saying anything, so Spencer decided to go for broke. He'd lay the groundwork on his project tonight, then elaborate at Christmas. Smiling at Mrs. Jordan, he said, "We're developing a robotic hand with tactile interface, which means the operator actually feels texture and temperature."

"How fascinating. Lexi, do you hear this?"

Lexi nodded.

"Tell me more, Dr. Price. How will people use your invention?"

"I can't take sole credit for the development. It's very much a group effort. We'd originally conceived applications for the hand in medicine and prosthetics, but we're expanding our scope every day," Spencer said.

"In what way?" Lawrence asked.

Any way you want, if it'll mean getting a grant. Spencer spoke a few more sentences designed to reveal both his project and to establish himself as the sort of man any sane parents would want courting their daughter. He'd had to sell his projects many times before. It wasn't too difficult to add himself to the package.

"Dr. Price, you sound as though you're accomplishing wonderful things with your life," Lexi's father said.

"Your parents must be very proud," her mother added.

Spencer smiled tightly.

Mrs. Jordan frowned at her daughter, then pushed Lexi's hair behind her ears. "You have such a pretty face, but with all that hair no one can see it."

"Mother." Lexi untucked her hair.

"Don't let her impersonation of a lounge lizard fool you, Dr. Price. Our Alexandra has a lot of talent." Mrs. Jordan smiled briefly. "Perhaps some day, when she chooses to exercise it, she'll accomplish great things, too."

Ouch. "I agree that she has talent. In fact, I just spent an enjoyable twenty minutes listening to her exercise it."

He might not have spoken.

"It isn't as though no one else in the family has ever achieved greatness," Mrs. Jordan went on. "My niece is Emily DeSalvo." She made the pronouncement with audible pride.

Spencer shook his head slightly. They'd just insulted Lexi. He wouldn't have acted impressed even if he'd known who Emily whatever her name was.

Mrs. Jordan raised her eyebrows. "The *opera* singer?"

Didn't he and Lexi have a conversation about opera? "I'm not much of an opera fan."

Lexi's mother looked huffy. "And I'm not a baseball fan, but even I know who Mickey Mantle was." She looked to her husband, who was nodding in agreement.

Right. It looked like the lab was going to get a dose of opera over the intercom in the next couple of weeks.

"Spencer has been involved with his research, Mom. He hasn't had time to follow Emily's career." Lexi finally spoke. "You'll get to meet her," she continued in an aside to him. "She's coming to Christmas dinner."

And you're overjoyed, aren't you? Spencer was beginning to get a feel for the Jordan family dynamics.

He hoped they believed in spiking the eggnog.

"Christmas dinner? Alexandra?" Her mother's eyebrows still arched upward.

Spencer held out his hand to Lexi. As she slipped her hand into his, he said, "Yes. Lexi extended your kind invitation to Christmas dinner. Thank you. I'll look forward to it."

"You asked Dr. Price to Christmas dinner?" A delighted Mrs. Jordan clasped her hands together, apparently forgiving him for not knowing her niece. "Oh, Alexandra, how very clever of you. Lawrence, Dr. Price will be coming to Christmas dinner."

Lawrence Jordan smiled benevolently. "Good. You can tell us more about your project."

Music to Spence's ears. He tugged gently on Lexi's hand, felt a brief resistance, then she stepped close enough for him to smile down at her.

When he met her mother's eyes again, Mrs. Jordan looked happily dazzled. Lawrence wore a proud-papa smile. Okay, mission accomplished. Except that Lexi seemed subdued, even for her.

"Lexi and I haven't had a chance to discuss the timing," Spencer said. "I'll be driving from my family's home in Dallas that morning. I can be at your house by one o'clock. Will that fit your schedule?" He'd managed to work his arm around Lexi's waist, presenting a Lexi-and-Spencer-are-a-couple picture to her parents.

He hoped Lexi noticed.

"One o'clock will be just about the time the goose is cooked." Mrs. Jordan beamed at them. "Oh, this is going to be the most wonderful Christmas!"

Lexi managed the most pitiful excuse for a smile Spencer had ever seen. She was going to have to fake it better than that if she wanted her parents to think they were an item.

"It's time for me to play my next set, or *my* goose will be cooked," she said.

"And we must be going, too," her mother said. "Lovely to meet you, Dr. Price. We'll look forward to seeing you at Christmas." After bestowing another smile on Spencer, Lexi's parents began a stately stroll toward the wine cellar.

Lexi pulled away from Spencer. "Thanks. You were great."

"Then why don't you look happy?"

"Oh…" She looked after her parents. "I let them get to me sometimes. They don't like me playing here."

"I gathered that."

"Anyway, it doesn't matter." She gave him a determined smile and changed the subject. "So, we were talking pool. It'll either have to be tomorrow, or next week. I'm booked for the weekend."

Spencer felt a pang of disappointment. "Dates?"

"Music gigs."

He had no business feeling so pleased. "Tomorrow is fine with me," Spencer said, finding that he was looking forward to seeing Lexi again.

"I'll need to check my calendar. With all the extra rehearsals, I've been rescheduling students right and left. Shall I call you tomorrow morning?"

"Sure." Once again, she was taking the upper hand, but it sounded so logical, Spencer couldn't object. Still, it rankled.

"I'll see you then." She started to walk off.

"Wait a sec." A glance toward the door revealed Lexi's parents standing in the restaurant foyer, within view. "How close do you want your parents to think we are?"

She glanced in the same direction. "They're so impressed with you, the closer we are, the better I look."

Spencer raised his hand and moved her hair back from her forehead. "This should do it, then."

And he kissed her. Right there in the main dining room of the Wainright Inn.

He figured surprise held her immobile, which was probably a good thing since he was nearly as surprised, himself. The gentle fusing of her lips against his sent shock waves through his body.

He'd been aiming for a kiss with a little more punch than a social peck on the cheek in a public place. He wanted a kiss that flirted with the edge of impropriety. A full kiss on the lips, then a lingering look as they reluctantly parted. A kiss that whispered of deeper intimacy.

Well, this kiss shouted deeper intimacy, if not past, then definitely future.

And a not-so-distant future at that.

He felt her hair swirl over his hand as it cupped the back of her head, felt her surprise soften, felt her lean closer.

Spencer decided to count the leaning closer as encouragement and angled his mouth over hers.

She was exactly the right height. His hand fit naturally at the small of her back—so naturally he didn't remember consciously putting it there, just as he didn't notice the precise instant when her hands loosed their grip on his arms and stole around his waist.

He inhaled, and a faint, exotic scent tantalized his nose. Her perfume wasn't the light floral he'd expected but a heavy, complex scent, lightly applied.

She'd probably dabbed it behind her ears, and only those privileged to get close to her would ever enjoy the scent. He inhaled again, finding that the deeper he breathed, the more layers were revealed. Probably like the woman, herself.

Hidden riches he was thinking just as there was a tap on his shoulder and a feminine throat cleared.

"We're late starting the next set."

Lexi jerked back, and stared at him, her eyes wide. Beside her stood Francesca, giving him a look that was simultaneously admiring and chastising.

"Call me," Spencer said, chagrined to hear a hoarse whisper instead of a sexy baritone.

Lexi opened her mouth, but nothing came out.

"If she won't, I will," Francesca said, before taking Lexi by the arm and leading her away. As they walked toward the platform by the windows, Spencer heard Francesca say, "I am definitely giving cotton a try."

"It smells wonderful in here." Francesca walked into the kitchen and stole a cookie.

"Frankie! Those are for the guys at the lab." Lexi had just pulled the last sheet of cookies out of the oven, and to make room, had to push aside the papers she was grading at the kitchen table.

"Spencer's lab?"

Lexi nodded.

Francesca waved over the counter where Lexi had dozens of chocolate-chip cookies cooling. "It's not like you don't have enough." As she munched, she scanned the cookies. "This batch by the sink has burnt edges. Rejects, right?"

Lexi nodded. "I got a phone call from Mom raving about Spencer, and they cooked too long."

And *raving* was an understatement. Her parents were acting as if nabbing an appropriate dinner partner for Christmas was the most wonderful thing Lexi had ever done. And in their eyes, Lexi supposed it must be.

"Mmm." Francesca held one of the burnt cookies over the sink and scraped the bottom with a knife. "Why are you doing this?"

"Spencer wowed my parents and I want to say thanks. And—" she sighed "—encourage him *not* to bail out before Christmas." To that end, Lexi had remembered to call *Texas Men*, but she hadn't yet recopied the letter. It couldn't be mailed before next week anyway.

"Cookies? You're thanking the man with cookies after you stood in the middle of Wainright's dining room and tickled his tonsils?"

"It wasn't like that. He just kissed me goodbye so my parents would think we have something going."

"You've definitely got something going. You two sizzled so much, I expected to see scorch marks on the carpet."

Yes, well, the kiss. Since Lexi had been thinking about her parents, she'd been caught completely off guard. Then when she realized he was kissing her, there were still a few Mr. December thoughts she had to get past before registering him as a man. A man with a warm mouth that did things that her parents couldn't possibly see from the restaurant foyer. Things that threatened to make her knees give way.

So that was when and why she'd clutched his

arms—to keep from falling if her knees buckled. It was perfectly understandable that he would think she wanted to turn up the heat of their kiss.

Her mind was the only part of her body that knew the kiss was just for show, and her mind wasn't being very helpful. It kept replaying those few moments in Spencer's arms until Lexi could think of little else.

And she was supposed to play pool with him tonight. Like the coward she was, she'd called before breakfast and left a message on his voice mail telling him she'd meet him at the lab. If it wasn't okay, he was supposed to call her back. He hadn't.

"I think the sizzling was completely one-sided," she admitted to Francesca, hoping her roommate would loyally contradict her.

She didn't. "Aha! So you admit you're attracted to him!"

"Frankie, if I told you I didn't find that man attractive, you'd have to call 911, because I wouldn't have a pulse."

"But there's attractive…and then there's *attractive.*"

Lexi knew exactly what she meant, which was why she was baking cookies. Cookies sent a casual and platonic message. A "Don't worry, I didn't take the kiss seriously" message.

In fact, that was probably just a casual kiss on his part and she was the one blowing everything out of proportion.

Which meant that his real kisses were…

Lexi stuffed a cookie into her mouth so Francesca would think her moan was due to chocolate bliss and not thoughts of Spencer.

"When are you taking these to the lab?" Francesca asked.

Swallowing, Lexi checked her watch. "In about forty-five minutes. Spencer is going to teach me to shoot pool at Busters."

"*Is* he? What are you going to wear?"

"This." Lexi gestured to her jeans and her Little-tree Music Department sweatshirt.

"You're joking."

"What's wrong with what I'm wearing? It's a casual beer-and-peanuts kind of place."

"You should be wearing a black leather miniskirt, fishnet stockings and boots. Come on, Lexi. It's like a rule."

"I'm going to be bending over a pool table!"

"I know."

"Even if I had a black leather miniskirt, I wouldn't wear it. That's too obvious."

"Let me see your shoes."

Lexi stuck out her foot.

"*Penny* loafers? I swear, you are the only grown woman I know who wears penny loafers."

"They're comfortable."

"You don't want comfortable, you want something that looks good. Now, you can wear the jeans if you wear spike heels and change into a sweater two sizes smaller."

"I don't have a sweater two sizes smaller."

Francesca got a sly look on her face. "Then we'll have to fill out one you do have."

"What are you talking about?"

"I'm talking about padding. What do you think I'm talking about? Come here."

What now? Lexi followed Francesca into her room.

"Look at this." She opened a drawer and took out a box. Inside were two flesh-colored blobs.

Lexi had a bad feeling about those blobs. "What are those?"

Francesca handed her one. "Fake boobs."

The blob was cold and squishy. "Ewww." Lexi dropped it back into its cream velvet nest.

"State-of-the-art," Francesca said. "They warm to your body temperature and conform to your shape. They feel like the real thing, so when you brush up against Spencer as he's demonstrating how to hold the pool cue, they'll feel real." As she talked, she opened another drawer and got out a bra.

"What is that? A cantaloupe carrier?"

Francesca laughed. "First you put in the demi-pads, then the breasts and then you."

"No thanks," Lexi said. "I'd bend over the pool table and lose my balance."

"Lexi, I'm telling you—"

"I know, I know. Underwear makes all the difference." She tried to visualize herself wearing the fake breasts and shook her head.

Francesca reluctantly put away her state-of-the-art padding. "By the way, I ordered the Egyptian cotton, but it won't come in until next week. Look, at least change tops, okay? And maybe wear boots instead of the loafers?"

Lexi had to change three more times before Francesca was satisfied, and then she was running late. "This sweater won't stay tucked in."

Francesca touched her hand to her cheek in mock dismay. "You mean it might come untucked and show a couple of inches of skin when you lean over to put the eight ball in the corner pocket? My, my."

Lexi gave her a look and headed for the kitchen. "I've got barely enough time to box up the cookies!"

"I'll help," Francesca offered. "In fact...Lexi, let me go with you. I want to meet the calendar cuties. Please?"

Francesca was expecting a lab full of living fantasies, which they weren't. Actually, Lexi thought she liked them better the way they were. "I don't think that's a good idea." She lined one of Francesca's underwear delivery boxes with foil and started putting the cookies into it.

"Why not? Are you ashamed of me?"

She should have known Francesca would argue. "No."

"You're afraid I'll make a play for Spencer, aren't you?" Her lower lip stuck out. "What kind of friend do you think I am?"

"It's not you, it's them. I know you're expecting these hunks, but they're not like that. They don't look like their pictures."

Francesca didn't believe her. "If they're even half as good-looking as Spencer, then I'll be thrilled."

"If you really mean that, then you can come. But I have to warn you, there has been a heck of a lot of retouching on their pictures."

"Even *my* picture was retouched. But there has to be something to retouch," Francesca said, walking to her room. Her voice drifted back to Lexi. "I'm changing into my cobalt-blue cat suit, so I'll be ice-cool sexy. Besides, it matches my toenail polish."

THEY DROVE to the lab in Lexi's car. For someone who had been so hot to trot about meeting the Science Hunks Calendar men, Francesca certainly acted very cool as they walked down the hallway leading to the lab.

Maybe there was something to underwear psychology after all.

Lexi had to admit—she looked good. In fact they looked good together. Frankie's hair was honey blond and as curly as Lexi's was straight. She was curvy where Lexi was slender, but Lexi was taller, where Francesca had to wear heels most of the time.

Lexi was suddenly glad that she'd worn the boots Francesca had insisted on.

They paused outside the door. "Do you want a drum roll?" Lexi asked.

Francesca tossed her head and licked her lips. "I'm ready."

Lexi opened the door and Francesca glided inside, then stood, surveying the room. Lexi, carrying the box of cookies, anxiously looked for the men.

A couple of them were at a long table filled with metal and wire. The others were wearing headphones and staring at computer monitors. A light spilled from Spencer's office doorway.

Murray was the first to notice them. He stared, then slid his headphones off his ears and slowly stood. Taking two steps forward, he was brought up short by the headphones still around his neck.

His actions caught the attention of some of the others until they were all staring at Lexi and Francesca.

Or make that staring at Francesca.

She wore a cool little smile and stared back.

"Hi, guys," Lexi said. "This is my roommate, Francesca."

"Hello, Francesca," they chorused in unison.

She wiggled her fingers.

"Lexi, is that you?" Spencer stuck his head out of the doorway. "I'll be another couple of minutes." He noticed Francesca, then looked at his fellow researchers, who'd apparently turned into zombies. "Oooh, boy."

Lexi walked over to him. "I brought you cookies to say thanks for charming my parents."

He nodded toward Francesca. "That's not all you brought."

"She wanted to come over here. I hope that's okay."

Spencer was still watching. "I don't know yet."

Lexi pried off the box lid. An aroma of chocolate and vanilla wafted out. "Want a cookie?"

"Not before..." Spencer sniffed. "Homemade?"

"You betcha. The ones on top are still warm."

Spencer popped one into his mouth, took another and then the entire box, which he carried to the snack area. "Hey, troops, Lexi made us cookies."

That seemed to break their spell.

"No kiddin'?" Murmuring their thanks, they seemed to come back to life.

Everyone, except Francesca, shuffled back to the snack area. Francesca did not shuffle. Francesca *un-dulated*. Undulated on high-heeled sandals.

Sandals in December? Her roommate was nutty, Lexi thought.

On the other hand, every eye in the place, including Spencer's, watched her progress. Francesca hopped onto the counter and crossed her legs. Within moments, a soft drink appeared in her hand.

"Why, thank you," Francesca drawled in a Southern belle voice.

Since she'd come from Indiana, this was totally fake, but Lexi doubted anyone noticed.

"Now, which month were you?" she asked Murray, who'd given her the drink.

"March and August."

"You shaved off your beard!"

Murray rubbed his day-old beard. "I'm growing it back."

"Oh, but why? With the beard, I didn't realize what a sexy mouth you have. That full lower lip just makes me want to..." She broke off with a self-deprecating laugh. "Sorry. I got a little carried away."

"I don't mind!" Murray said quickly.

"Did you want something else to drink?" asked one of the others.

"Or a cookie?"

"I've got chips over here."

"And doughnuts—"

"Not those, man!"

Francesca laughed and swung her leg back and forth as they crowded around her. "I know you— you're July!"

There was more laughter as the men visibly relaxed.

"Your roommate's all right," Spencer murmured in Lexi's ear.

"Yeah, she is." Lexi caught Frankie's eye and gave her a thumbs-up sign.

Francesca grinned.

"You want to slip out now?" Spencer asked.

"I thought you weren't ready to leave yet."

Spencer looked down at her, and a slow smile warmed his eyes. "That's before I saw you."

6

BUSTERS MANAGED TO BE both bright and dark at the same time. Since Rocky Falls catered to tourists, all the businesses had a clean-scrubbed veneer and Busters was no different.

College kids crowded the tables and dropped peanut shells on the floor. An old-fashioned jukebox played country-Western music.

The pool tables were in the back. Spencer took her hand as he led Lexi past the booths. She spotted several of her students who gave her exaggerated signals that they approved of Spencer.

There was no hope that he hadn't noticed.

"Shouldn't you be practicing?" she scolded them good-naturedly as she walked past.

The truth was, Spencer couldn't help attracting attention. He had a commanding presence, not to mention that his picture was probably on display in every dorm room at Littletree right now.

He was a decade older than some of the young males sitting in the booths, and it showed in the confident way he moved, the firm line of his jaw and his filled-out shoulders. In contrast, most of the male students couldn't yet grow a full beard.

Put Spencer next to them, and, well, Spencer was very much a man.

And Lexi found that she didn't like the assessing

looks he was drawing from the college women. Walking faster, she closed the gap between them.

He grinned down at her and marginally slowed his stride.

Take that, you college nymphettes.

The pool room was quieter, since it was located away from the music and the electronic beeping of the video games. There was a faint smoky smell but overall, it added to the atmosphere without being objectionable.

"I reserved a table," Spencer told her, "but we're early. What can I get you to drink? You can have anything you like, but I'm hoping you won't go white wine on me."

Lexi laughed. "Nope. How about a beer?"

"Good choice." He turned her around so she faced the wall. "Now all you have to do is decide which one. There's the menu."

Hanging on the back wall of the pool room was a gigantic wooden plaque on which had been shellacked the labels of at least two hundred kinds of beer.

"Texas is loaded with microbreweries. You ought to give some of them a shot."

"I will. It'll be like finding undiscovered talent."

They passed the next several minutes discussing the merits of various flavors, whether Lexi preferred a "full" flavor, dark, lager, stout, even raspberry flavored.

The thought of raspberries in beer gave Lexi a few queasy moments. "I give up. Pick me something that goes with peanuts—unsalted peanuts." She peered closer. "Wait a minute, have you ever had that one?" She pointed to a splotch of wild color amid the browns, golds and tans.

"Yeah." Spencer seemed to approve of her choice. "I like it a lot. What made you choose it?"

"There's a psychedelic longhorn on the label. I figure that took guts, so it must be a gutsy beer."

"I suppose that's one way to describe the flavor."

Spencer ordered two bottles of the beer, then he and Lexi sat on bar stools and watched the pool games in progress. She felt far more relaxed with him than she'd anticipated, considering neither of them had referred to the humdinger of a kiss they'd shared last night. Probably because for Spencer, it had neither hummed, nor dinged.

Lexi sighed inwardly as she reluctantly doused the little flare of hope for a closer relationship with Spencer—the one her parents thought she had.

It was funny how they could influence her thinking. Her cousin Emily who had found the perfect man notwithstanding, Lexi had found committed relationships difficult to maintain when both partners had strong goals that threatened to take them in different directions. A relationship took work, and Lexi had eventually realized she was the one who was expected to make all the sacrifices for its sake.

Maybe someday she'd be ready, but she supposed she was too selfish right now. She had a lot she wanted to accomplish before she put another person's desires and needs ahead of her own.

She remembered the first time she'd been expected to choose between her music and a man. He hadn't been a musician and couldn't understand that she needed uninterrupted time to practice. It wasn't that she loved music more than him, but realized his impatience was a clue to their future. The relationship was doomed. Music wasn't the culprit. He couldn't accept that she had something equally as important in her life as he was.

Spencer was probably the same way. Just watching his face as he talked about the mechanical hand he was designing told her the project meant everything to him.

Not much room in his life for anything—or anyone—else.

Lexi understood. She even agreed with him. So she should quit whining about what she didn't have and be grateful for what she did have—a nice, casual evening out with an intelligent man who was easy on the eyes.

And the beer wasn't bad, either. She took another sip. It had a full beefy flavor with an unexpectedly zingy aftertaste—just like the label.

Spencer cracked open a peanut. "So how much do you know about pool?"

"I have no idea of the rules, except that when the cue ball leaves the table, it's a bad thing."

"That's right. You don't want it to go into a pocket."

"No, I mean bouncing off the table."

"Ah." Spencer rubbed behind his neck. "How old were you when you did that?"

"Eight. It hit the concrete floor in the basement and chipped. Grandfather never let me play after that."

"That happens to all of us at one time or another."

"Maybe not at the same time you break the Tiffany lamp over the table with the pool cue."

"You did that too?"

"Only because Les—that's my twin brother—spilled his cherry Kool-Aid over my hand."

Spencer winced. "Was your hand on the table at the time?"

"Of course. I was trying to shoot."

"That's when the ball went bouncing off the table."

"And I jerked up and hit the lamp with the cue."

Nodding, Spencer said, "I see your grandfather's point."

They ate peanuts, sipped their beer and chatted about inconsequentials until a bell sounded, signaling the end of the pool session.

"We're at table three." Spencer indicated the one just in front of them. "Let's choose you a cue."

Ninety percent of the cues racked on the wall were the same length, so Lexi didn't see that there was much choice. However, Spencer examined several, looking down their length, testing their flexibility and weight.

"You must play a lot of pool," Lexi commented.

"Not really. Just trying to impress you."

"Give me that!" Lexi laughed and grabbed for the cue he held.

"I suppose you're going to want this, too." In his hand, he held a small blue square.

"Definitely. Chalking the cue was my favorite part. We'd use the chalk after every shot and make piles of blue dust."

Spencer shuddered in mock horror as he racked the balls and positioned the point of the triangle over a well-worn spot on the table. "Your poor grandfather."

"Actually, Grandmother cleaned up the mess. Do I get to break?" she asked.

"Not literally."

Lexi was still laughing, now utterly at ease with Spencer. So when she positioned the cue ball, then bent over the table trying to remember how to hold the cue, she wasn't anticipating her reaction when Spencer ever so casually leaned over her to correct her position.

It was a heart-jarring shock when her body went from buddy-buddy mode to full sexual awareness in a fraction of a second.

The distinctive click as the balls cracked into each other, the murmurs of the other players and the music all faded away as Lexi's complete sensory attention was focused on Spencer and his nearness to her.

Part of her back was flush against his chest, the same chest that greeted her each morning. Funny how his fingers no longer had quite the same allure, though there they were, in the lamplight, tangling with hers.

His cheek, with the faint shadow of beard, was inches away. He was telling her something, but she was registering only the vibrations his voice made against her back. She shifted her position, bringing more of him in contact with her body.

"No, like this." He leaned over farther as he placed her rubbery fingers around the pool cue. Her right hip and thigh now met his. The bottom edge of her sweater pulled out of the waist of her jeans, exposing a couple of inches of skin.

He leaned down, trying to get to her eye level to line up the shot, saying something about physics and geometry, concepts her mind couldn't quite grasp at this moment.

"Got it?"

Well, no. If she could only find a way to indicate that he needed to adjust her position, maybe by putting those long fingers in direct contact with her waist—

"Okay, now shoot."

"Do I have to?"

He chuckled and she smiled as the deep rumbles caressed her back. "I've got a hold of the back end here," he said. "Don't worry."

Lexi sighed. All good things must come to an end.

Just then, Spencer gently traced the edge of her hair over her temple and lifted it behind her shoulder, making a whole new area of her body aware of him. Tingles zinged down the side of her neck and lodged in her elbow.

Her muscles wouldn't respond. But they had to, or he'd guess what was wrong.

Sharply pulling the pool cue back, she horribly overcompensated and heard the "oomph" sound Spencer made when the cue met his stomach—or worse.

She missed the cue ball completely.

"Ohmigosh!" She jerked upright and her head crunched against his.

Lexi whirled around.

Blinking rapidly, Spencer hunched over and held his hands over his nose.

"Oh…I'm so sorry!" Before she realized what she was doing, she found herself rubbing his stomach about where she judged the cue's point of impact to be.

"Too high."

She moved her hand lower.

Inhaling, he grabbed her wrist. "Still too high, but thanks for the thought." His voice sounded stuffy.

"Your nose! I'm so sorry! Should I get an ice pack from the bartender?"

"Nah. I'll be okay." Gingerly he explored the contours of his nose, then squinted at her. "You mind if we sit for a few minutes?"

"Of course not!" Lexi searched for an empty table or booth. "Those people are leaving." She grabbed the bottles of beer, and stood by the booth until the waiter had swiped off the peanut shells.

Spencer gingerly slid across the vinyl seat. "Pool isn't your game, is it?"

"But it could be." Lexi sat across from him. "I want it to be. That was just a silly mistake. The cue stuck against my fingers, or something." As she looked at him, an angry red spot marking the impact site of her head was forming above the bridge of his nose.

She wondered where the pool cue had hit.

She wished she'd worn a tight low-cut sweater and Francesca's fake breasts to take his mind off the pain.

Except that might cause more pain in the area of the cue mishap, so it was probably just as well that she was sitting across from him "unenhanced."

"What are you thinking?" he asked her.

"Why?"

"You have the weirdest expression on your face."

"Well, I'm—" *not going to tell you about Francesca's breasts* "—I'm horrified and embarrassed."

"Don't be." He waved away her words and gave

her a smile whose potency wasn't diminished one bit by his slightly swollen nose. Withdrawing a folded piece of paper from his pocket, he sniffed and said, "We needed to talk about a few things, anyway."

He unfolded the paper and Lexi saw that it was a checklist.

"I think I made a good impression on your parents," he said questioningly.

"That's an understatement."

At her dry tone, he glanced up from reading the list. "I thought that was the whole idea."

"Yes."

"But...?"

With her thumb, Lexi traced the damp outline of the longhorn on her beer bottle. How was she supposed to tell him her parents thought he was the greatest achievement of her life? That she hadn't realized how much she'd wanted to see the pleased approval on their faces until then? And what was it that they approved of? Him. None of her accomplishments mattered. In fact, it was obvious that her mother didn't consider Lexi worthy of Spencer.

She hadn't expected the knowledge to hurt as much as it did. "I guess that until last night, I hadn't realized my parents considered me deficient without a man," she told Spencer.

He appeared to give her words serious thought. "Do they have any grandchildren?"

Lexi shook her head.

"That's probably it. They've just got grandchild fever."

Even though Lexi hadn't ever heard her mother talk about wanting grandchildren as anything other than ammunition against the two Emily had presented to Aunt Carolyn, Lexi let his reasoning slide by. She'd already gone wading in the pool of embarrassment this evening. No need to go scuba diving.

He took out a pen. "I need some information about you. Brothers and sisters?"

"A brother, Les—"

"The twin, right." Spencer wrote down the name. "I'm trying to picture a male version of you, and I can't."

"That's okay. We're not identical," she said with a straight face.

He started to write, then looked at her from under his eyebrows. "Very funny."

"People do ask."

"Mmm. Just you and your brother?"

Lexi drew a deep breath. "Unfortunately, no. There's Gretchen, my little sister. She's the reason for the family gathering."

She looked at Spencer diligently making notes and thought about how obviously busy he was, yet he'd taken not one, but two evenings of his time to get to know her. All she'd asked of him was that he show up on Christmas, but he'd figured out a lot more was required. Had he complained? Had he cried foul? Had he said, "Forget it!" because he'd already met her father? No, he'd set out to do the best job he could.

And she was leading him right into Norman Rockwell as interpreted by Salvador Dali.

Moaning, Lexi put her head in her hands. "I can't stand the guilt any longer. I've got to tell you what you're getting into." She met his eyes. "This is going to be the worst Christmas of your life."

Not a chance.

The Christmas he'd walked back from the bus station in the dark to his boarding school dormitory was the worst. He'd had to break a window to get back inside because the whole school was shut down for the holidays. He'd left the window unlocked, but the ever-vigilant custodian, Mr. Sayers, must have discovered it during a final check.

All the students had either gone home, or had made arrangements to spend the holidays with friends. Spencer had neither, but he wasn't about to admit it, so he'd packed enough clothing to allay suspicion and had accepted a ride to the bus station where he'd spent most of Christmas Eve. When he felt it was safe to return, he'd done so. Once he'd broken into the building, he'd spent a cold holiday, since the heat had been cut off, something he hadn't reckoned on.

The day after New Year's, he'd packed once more, then sat on the steps outside and waited for the returning headmaster. The memory was one he'd like to forget.

"It's going to be a great Christmas," he said now. "I'm looking forward to it." And had been since he'd kissed her last night. It would be interesting to experience a real family Christmas dinner.

Not that his foster family wasn't real to him, but he'd always been curious about what being with a regular family at Christmas would be like.

"You don't understand—this whole family thing was Gretchen's therapist's idea. Knowing Gretchen, she'll go out of her way to be the center of attention. And Les's mission in life is to successfully rebel. Thus far he's failed, so I'm sure he'll be in a cranky mood. My mother and my aunt Carolyn have a rivalry going and my exalted cousin Emily is taking time off from her fabulous operatic career to grace us with her presence. She's bringing her adoring husband and her perfectly behaved children.''

It all sounded great to Spencer.

"To top it off, my mom is obsessed. The day will be a combination of Betty Crocker and Martha Stewart, with highlights from *The Nutcracker* and *A Christmas Carol* thrown in." She sighed. "God bless us, every one."

Spencer had been writing as she talked. "I think I have all your relatives. Sounds like an intriguing bunch."

She raised a black eyebrow over those incredible blue eyes. "You really are an optimist, aren't you?"

"One of us has to be."

He would not look at her incredible blue eyes. He would not think of how she felt pressed against his chest. He would not think of her leg alongside his. He would not breathe in her fancy perfume and speculate on what other areas of her body she'd placed it. He'd been thinking of all that before, and now he'd probably end up with a black eye and his future children would be born with headaches.

He moved to the next item on the list. "What should I bring to make a good impression?"

"You mean I haven't scared you off?"

"Nope."

"Well, then." She tossed her hair over her shoulder and he watched it ripple down to her waist. "If you really want to make an impression, bring a smoked turkey or a ham."

"But I thought your mother said you were having goose."

"I have a bad feeling about the goose. Mother isn't much of a hands-on cook and, I don't know. Call it a hunch. By the time you get there, a smoked turkey might be very much appreciated."

"You don't think a pie or a bottle of wine—"

"Trust me. Smoked turkey."

"If you say so." He had his doubts, but she knew best. Spencer made a note to pick up a bottle of wine just in case.

As he moved down his list, he learned more and more about her, painting in her character as he went.

Surprisingly enough, he was using brights when he'd expected to use pastels. She had definite opinions, but they had to be drawn out of her. She wasn't one to spout off just for the sake of hearing herself speak.

The more he dug, the more he found he liked. She was passionate about her music, which meant she could be passionate in other areas, as well. Always nice to know. And she had plans. He liked a woman with plans. Women with plans didn't depend on him to provide the focus for their lives.

He'd been in clingy relationships before, but not for long. In fact he hated the word *relationship*. It usually meant expectations on the part of the woman, and Spencer didn't have time for that now.

He was enjoying the evening, in spite of their earlier pool efforts, and then she asked him about his family.

It was a logical question, but Spencer didn't want to discuss his background. He had a dozen stories he could tell her, all of them fabrications. But he found that he didn't want to lie to Lexi, and yet he wasn't ready to tell her everything, either. He'd never told anybody everything, not even the guys at the lab.

"No brothers, no sisters," he said abruptly. "My folks retired on a couple of acres outside of Dallas. You want to try a game of pool now?"

Thankfully she allowed the change of subject. "You sure are brave."

They managed one game of pool without further mishap. Lexi probably would have had better luck if Spencer had helped her line up her shots, but every time she bent over the pool table, the curtain of her hair fell over her shoulder, and her sweater rode up to reveal a tantalizing sliver of skin as white as the cue ball. Normally he'd enjoy the sight. A lot. But now when Spencer's heart kicked up a notch, the blood pounded in his head—not to mention elsewhere—making it hurt.

So in the interests of physical comfort, he found one game to be all he could stand. It was just as well. Tomorrow was a workday and Lexi not only had an early morning class, she was also performing at the Wainright Inn later in the day.

Spencer found himself mentally toying with the idea of coming to see her again.

There was something about her that drew him and, though he'd found her initially attractive, he hadn't expected to like her. At first she'd reminded him too much of the prep school kids who'd looked down on him. But after tonight the resemblance had faded.

She'd brought them all cookies. Homemade cookies. After a kiss like the one they'd exchanged, he hadn't figured her for a homemade cookie type.

Which meant she was more complex than he'd figured.

Yeah, he ought to see her again before Christmas.

Driving along in his car, Lexi directed him across Main Street toward her house. As the car climbed the gentle hill, Spencer automatically looked toward his left. It was the only view in town that cleared the falls to the other side. In the distance, for a fraction of a second, he'd be able to see the research building. Since the falls were lit up at night, the reflection of colored lights in the churning water would give the building a moving tie-dyed effect.

He slowed, so he could point it out to Lexi, then stopped the car and stared.

"What's the matter?"

"I was going to show you the research building. It looks cool at night, but there are lights on in the lab."

"Is that unusual?"

Unusual enough to make him nervous. He hoped there hadn't been a break-in. Spencer automatically checked his watch. "Rip mostly works at night, but he doesn't like a lot of light."

"Do you want to check it out?"

Spencer looked down at her. "Do you mind?"

She shook her head, and Spencer didn't ask her twice.

THEY WERE IN the hallway outside the lab doors when Spencer cocked his head. "Is that a cello?"

Lexi knew the piece. She'd listened to her roommate practice it. "And not just any cello," she said.

"Francesca must still be here. That's strange. I left my car for her to use, but I didn't see it in the lot."

"What are they doing?" Spencer muttered, opening the door.

Lexi didn't know what she expected, but it wasn't finding her roommate hooked up to a bunch of wires, concentrating fiercely as she played her cello.

Murray, a besotted look on his face, sat beside her. Gordon and another man whose name Lexi couldn't remember hovered around a computer station. Another sat in front of an oscilloscope, and the man with the thick glasses was studying printouts of squiggly lines as fast as they rolled out of the machine. Mr. October was off by himself at a computer, typing furiously and muttering to himself.

"What have they done to her?" she asked.

"They've got electrodes hooked up to her, so they're studying something." Spencer's voice had an absent quality that told Lexi he was concentrating on the scene in front of them. "It's got to do with the hand and it must be good."

"Why do you say that?"

He nodded toward Mr. October. "Because Rip is involved. He's a purist who doesn't believe in wasting his time."

Spencer started forward, attracting Murray's attention.

"Doc!" Everyone, except Rip, looked up and broke into an excited babble.

Francesca looked like she was a cat and they'd been feeding her cream.

"Hold it." Spencer held up a hand. "Murray, what's going on?"

"Whoa." He drew a deep breath and exhaled

heavily. "It's been incredible. We were showing Frankie the beta prototype of the hand and explaining about the tactile interface we wanted." He had to stop and draw another breath.

Francesca continued the explanation. "I told them how I can tell if I'm playing in tune by the vibration of the strings against my fingers. I can feel the pitch."

Spencer had an arrested look on his face. Lexi felt a twinge of jealousy which she mentally stamped out.

"So you've been trying to identify how her brain gave her that information and translate it into computer language." He practically ran over to the monitor, ignoring Francesca, which improved Lexi's frame of mind.

Until Spencer leaned over the desk, picked up a photo and shot a look at Francesca.

One glance at Francesca and Lexi knew which photo it was—the one where Francesca was all cello, legs and cleavage. The black-and white picture suggested more than revealed, and the curve of the cello was echoed by the curve of Francesca's body. It was a beautiful photograph.

Under ordinary circumstances, Lexi appreciated it as *Womancello*, part of the portfolio assembled by one of the art students.

But these weren't ordinary circumstances.

She narrowed her eyes and marched over to her roommate. "What do you think you're doing?" she asked in a low voice.

"I brought them a picture."

"Why?"

"Well, it seemed only fair since I'd been admiring

their pictures all year. Now they have one of me."
She looked entirely too pleased with herself.

"Very nice," Spencer said, and tossed the picture
back onto the table without another glance. "Rip?
How's it going?"

"Prime data," Rip answered, without looking up
from the monitor.

"I understand that's high praise," Francesca
whispered.

"Francesca, could you play again so I can see this
in action?" Spencer asked.

"Sure, Doc." As she positioned her bow, she said
to Lexi, "They call him Doc."

"I know that," Lexi said, but Francesca's playing
covered it up.

Lexi stood out of the way for several minutes.
Spencer didn't glance up once. Then she wandered
over to the snack bar and sat, noticing that only
cookie crumbs remained in the box she'd brought.
She'd really intended for Spencer to eat more of
them than he had, but obviously the others had enjoyed them, so it was okay. Sort of.

She tried not to be aware of how long she sat in
the cluttered snack bar watching Francesca be the
center of attention. When she attempted to clear
away some of the wrappers, they shushed her.

Being jealous of Francesca was silly. They were all
adults here, and this wasn't a contest. She should be
glad of the opportunity to watch Spencer in action,
even if most of the action consisted of him pointing
at a screen, gesturing to Francesca, yelling across the
room to Rip or running to look at Bob's—she was
learning their names—printout.

Bashful Bob, she thought. Every time he looked at

Francesca, he blushed. But Murray, the chemistry teacher at Littletree, openly adored her. Lexi hoped Francesca would let him down easily.

She'd go home, if she could, but Francesca had her car keys and Lexi wasn't sure where she'd parked the car.

One of Francesca's electrodes came undone and everyone gathered around her as Murray reattached it. "Are you okay? Can we get you something to drink?" he asked.

Nobody asked Lexi if she was thirsty, she grumbled to herself. In fact, it appeared they'd forgotten she was sitting back there.

"Hey, Rip—get us a Coke, okay?"

The tall, forbidding Mr. October uncoiled himself from his computer and dug in the pocket of his jeans for change. He turned and picked out two quarters before noticing her.

She saw the surprise on his face.

"I'd forgotten that you graced our presence, lovely one," he said as he punched the money into the machine.

"So has everyone else," Lexi said, hoping the whine stayed out of her voice.

Rip whistled. Murray held up a hand and Rip tossed him the canned drink before turning back to her. "Allow me to return you to home and hearth."

Go out alone with the Lord of the Night?

He smiled faintly at her hesitation. "Fear not. I've already supped this evening."

She was being ridiculous. Laughing, Lexi stood and slung her purse over her shoulder. "In that case, I accept."

Rip's car looked like the Batmobile, but was really a black Dodge Viper. It fit him.

"Thanks so much for taking the time to drive me home," she said as they left the parking lot. "It's not that I'm not fascinated by watching all of you in action, but I do have an early class tomorrow." She chattered brightly, nervous in spite of her resolve not to be.

They reached the exit gate. Rip pushed a card into the time clock and looked at her as the wooden barrier arm raised.

She saw his gaze sweep over her, but instead of feeling warmed as she had when Spencer had done virtually the same thing, she felt chilled.

"I really appreciate this," she reiterated because his silence bothered her. "Spencer told me that you don't like to waste time."

Rip smiled faintly. "He is correct. Where we differ is that I can recognize what is worth my time and what is not."

He was being kind. Relaxing for the first time in his presence, she told him so.

"Not at all," he said. "Spencer Price remains so focused on his goal of achieving validation through his design of the hand, that he fails to enjoy the journey. What he must realize is that spending time with a beautiful woman with skin like moonlight and hair as black as the night should be part of the journey."

7

FRANCESCA DIDN'T GET IN until three-thirty in the morning.

Lexi knew because she was still awake, fighting a losing battle to keep from feeling miffed.

She was being so juvenile. Unjustifiably juvenile. Transparently juvenile. Even Rip had seen through her.

Get over it, she told herself, finally falling asleep after she heard Francesca put her cello in the music room.

Naturally she overslept. Perfect. No coffee, no breakfast. But at least she wouldn't have to fake anything in front of Francesca, who was still asleep.

This was the last day of the semester before music classes were suspended for performance juries the following week. Francesca had left Lexi's car parked in the garage, safe and sound, which was a relief. She made it to the music building with a few minutes to spare. Racing up the stairs to her third-floor studio—as soon as she made full professor, she was putting in for one on the second floor—Lexi rounded the corner and stopped.

Sitting on the floor outside her door was Spencer and a gigantic red poinsettia.

He gave her a weary smile, his teeth very white against a day's growth of black beard. He still wore the same clothes he'd worn last night, so it wasn't hard to guess that he hadn't been home yet.

He looked great. "You're almost late for class, missy."

"I overslept," she admitted. "What are you doing here?"

He stood as she unlocked her door and followed her inside. "I come bearing gifts."

She dumped her portfolio on her desk and turned around.

Spencer held up a small bakery sack and the poinsettia. "If I recall, it's supposed to be a croissant and coffee—"

"Coffee!" she shrieked, reaching for the bag. "You brought me coffee? You angel!"

"I'm forgiven already?"

"Yes." She removed the foam cup from the bag and pried off the plastic lid. "Oh, yes, yes, yes, yes." She took a sip and closed her eyes. "I will live."

"Though it's not in my best interests to tell you this, you should have made me suffer more."

Lexi broke off a corner of the croissant. "More than a knock on the head and a jab—" her eyes lowered "—elsewhere?" She popped the flaky bread into her mouth. Fat-gram heaven.

"That wasn't anything. I'm over it."

Lexi elected not to mention the dark circles under his eyes. After all, they could be from lack of sleep.

Spencer set the poinsettia on her desk. "There. A bright wildflower. I picked it myself. Just for you."

Lexi swallowed. "Spencer? That's a poinsettia, and judging by the gold foil around the pot, I'd say it was domesticated."

"Domesticated wildflowers? Is nothing sacred?"

"Apparently not the decorations in the lobby."

He grinned and Lexi laughed. "You'd better take it back."

"I want you to have it. I'll replace the one downstairs."

She snapped the plastic cap back on her coffee and gathered the materials she needed for her class. "Actually, it would be better off downstairs. I kill plants. That's why I like wildflowers. I figure they've got a keen sense of self-preservation."

He laughed, then his smile faded. "You've got to get to class, I know, but I did want to apologize for abandoning you last night."

"I understand." And she did. Under similar circumstances, she would have done the same thing. "Did you get some good information from Francesca?"

Tired as he was, his eyes lit up and words poured out of him. Technical words that flew right past Lexi, but he was so obviously elated that she quit trying to understand him and just enjoyed watching him talk.

And she'd once thought his intelligence was only a trick of the photographer's light.

"It's a whole new way of looking at the tactile interface," he said, winding down. "I don't know why we hadn't thought of it before. Now we've got to scramble to incorporate this new information into our end-of-the-year reports and grant applications. We've got hours of data. Your roommate must have been exhausted, but she never complained. I've got to tell you, I have a completely different impression of her now."

"I'll bet," Lexi said, thinking of the picture.

Spencer must have been, too. "By the way, she's become the team mascot. They're blowing her picture up to poster size."

"She'll be thrilled," Lexi said through clenched teeth.

"Anyway, we appreciate her help."

"You ought to pick up a poinsettia for her."

He gazed at her. "Hey."

"What?" But Lexi knew her annoyance was showing.

"I'm sorry."

"It's okay. Rip took me home." She couldn't resist adding, "You know, he's a nice guy, but he tries to hide it. I enjoyed getting to know him a little bit."

Spencer's eyes flashed when she mentioned Rip. "But I would have kissed you good-night."

It was a good thing she'd put the lid back on the coffee, because she would have ended up wearing it. Amazing how a few words could completely change the atmosphere. A second ago, she'd been resentful of Francesca—and she still was—but Francesca was not here with Mr. December. Lexi was. And Mr. December had just told her she'd missed out on a good-night kiss. Now *there* was something to be upset about.

A smile touched his lips. "It's my opinion that our evening hasn't officially ended yet."

Lexi felt her eyes grow wide. She couldn't move. She couldn't speak, which was just as well, because she probably would have babbled, and babbling lips didn't get kissed.

But Spencer was talking instead of kissing, anyway. "The thing is, we're going to rewrite all our reports and I'll be working like a maniac for the next two weeks."

So focused on his goal of achieving validation... Uh-oh. This was not prelude-to-a-kiss talk. This was kiss-off talk.

"I can't promise I'll see you again before Christmas. I'll be working crazy hours, probably sleeping when you're awake—"

"It's okay." No, it wasn't, but she didn't want him to think she expected anything, even though she'd thought... But Rip had warned her, hadn't he? "You've already done far more than you needed to." She dug in her purse and handed him a slightly beat-up envelope. "I recopied your letter last night after I got home. Added some new stuff, too. You'll like it."

He slowly took it and stared down at the address. "I'd forgotten all about this."

But he couldn't have. That's why he was coming to... He was still coming to Christmas dinner, wasn't he? Maybe she shouldn't have given him the letter just yet.

"Thanks." He looked up at her. "I'm going to go home and hit the sack."

She laughed, surprised she could. "Good night, then. See you at Christmas," she added as a pointed reminder.

"Good night." But he didn't move away. Instead he gazed at her, at first questioning, then with unmistakable intent.

The air thickened around them.

Lexi actually blinked to make sure she wasn't hallucinating due to caffeine deprivation. Yes, it was a definite I-want-to-kiss-you-now look.

And her parents weren't anywhere around.

The man whom thousands of women were drooling over was standing in her cold studio about to kiss her. It would probably be just a platonic, good-bye kiss, but maybe she should knock her dates in the head more often.

He leaned forward, his arms going around her. "I haven't shaved."

"And I'm officially late for class."

If he accepted that excuse, he wasn't as bright as she thought he was.

Slowly, gently, he touched his mouth to hers, careful not to brush his beard against her. His lips were soft, warm, sensuous, tender...tantalizing.

And sweet... Oh so sweet.

Spencer's slow kiss kindled a warmth inside her that made her forget she was on the cold third floor, made her forget about classes, Christmas and posters of naked roommates.

A part of her knew that it wasn't supposed to be a swept-away sort of kiss, but it was hard to keep her footing during the emotional tidal wave he started. Still, she struggled.

Okay, not very hard.

Then he touched the corners of her mouth with the tip of his tongue and she happily realized that she didn't have to pretend this was a platonic kiss anymore, and could surrender to her feelings.

If a girl was going to surrender, she could do a lot worse, Lexi thought. She could also do a lot more.

He traced a series of tiny nipping kisses around her mouth until she shivered as her newly heated skin reacted to the cold air.

Her lips had never been this sensitive before.

They throbbed, they tingled and they magnified his touch. So when Spencer once again settled his mouth fully against hers, firmly, but still gently, Lexi felt the kiss all the way to her toes and back up again.

Spencer's kiss blew away every idea about passion she'd ever had. She'd never felt kissed so completely. Who knew gentle could be powerful? Who knew slow could be fast?

It was an intimate kiss. It was a sneaky kiss—deceptively simple, yet full of intensity.

It was a dangerously insidious kiss for a man to give a woman—because it was the kind of kiss that floated right past a girl's defenses and landed on her heart.

BUT KISS OR NO KISS, it looked as though Lexi wouldn't get to see Spencer before Christmas after all, unless she took drastic measures. He was as busy as he said he'd be. He'd called once, a distracted ramble where he verified the time he should arrive and asked directions to her parent's house.

Apparently her letter was a hit at *Texas Men.* He let her know how glad he was that he could finally concentrate on his project again. And that's what he was doing.

Francesca had a suggestion. It involved underwear, as always. "You've been tense lately," she said to Lexi from the doorway of the music room.

"It's a tense time of year." Lexi was at the piano trying to arrange their Christmas medleys so she could play them with Gwen, the harpist, while Francesca was in Indiana for the holidays.

"It's affecting your performance."

Lexi glanced up from the notes she was making. "I thought it was giving my playing an edge."

"'Silent Night' doesn't need an edge." Francesca walked into the room. "Seduce him."

Lexi didn't even pretend she hadn't been thinking the same thing. "He's busy."

"*Not* that busy."

"That busy. They all are—with tactile modifications for that stupid hand."

Francesca winced and pressed her fingers to her temple. "Hasn't living with me taught you anything?"

"Sure. Early to bed and early to rise means you're not wearing the right underwear."

"Very good, but that wasn't what I meant."

"It's not what you know, it's your underwear?"

Francesca looked heavenward. "I try to help and this is the thanks I get?"

Lexi was on a roll. "The love of underwear is the root of all—"

"Okay, Lexi. I'll just take your Christmas present—the one I paid extra to have sent overnight express—and let you continue to suffer, when with my help you might achieve a state of blissful relaxation, emphasis on the bliss." Francesca looked at the flat box in her hands and sighed.

Bliss could be good. "I'm sorry. I'm—I'm tense."

"And I'm leaving tomorrow. It'll be a perfect time for you to get a little less tense."

Easy for her to say. "But how am I supposed to pry Spencer away from that stupid hand?"

"You don't. Must I spell everything out?"

"Yes." Lexi picked up her pencil and turned over the sheet music. "I'll take notes."

"It's not complicated." Francesca began to pace. "When I stop by the lab to say goodbye and give the guys their presents, I'll tell Spencer that you volunteered to test the hand for him. They wanted me to, but I'll sacrifice."

"I don't play the cello."

"Don't tell him!" Francesca threw up her hand in frustration. "By the time he figures it out, he shouldn't care!"

"Oh."

"Now, Lexi, you'll have privacy, a piano, Spencer…and this." Francesca handed her the box. "Merry Christmas."

Lexi perked up. Francesca's presents were always unusual. "Thanks, Frankie. Should I open it now?" A rhetorical question. Lexi was already fingering the pull-tab on the box.

"Definitely yes."

Francesca had left the present in the cardboard delivery box. Lexi ripped that open, then found a shiny fuchsia padded gift envelope inside.

She opened that and dumped out the contents. Then she stared. "Is this leather underwear?"

"It's the biker chick ensemble." Francesca beamed, obviously terribly pleased with herself. "And look at all those zippers and chains. Ooo, and hidden hooks and snaps." She pulled one open. "The Gate of Delight. What fun!" She gave a little shimmy. "I ordered a set for me in red, but they're out of stock."

"The Gate of— I don't think I'm ready for leather underwear."

"If all goes well, you won't have to wear it long." Francesca gave her an exaggerated wink.

Lexi held up the briefs with the back zippers. "This gives visible panty line a whole new meaning."

"Spencer likes gadgets, so the underwear should appeal to him." Francesca grinned. "And what a test for the mechanical hand. If it passes, then you both win."

SPENCER WAS RUNNING late. Lexi had been awfully understanding when he'd asked if she'd help him test the hand. He wanted a musician's opinion, and with Francesca out of town, Lexi was the only musician he knew. He felt like he was taking advantage of her, but Francesca had seemed to think she wouldn't mind.

He had to ring the doorbell with his shoulder because he was carrying so much equipment. The prototype still had breadboards attached, and that kind of temporary circuit didn't transport well. He'd probably have to reattach wires before they could test it.

He could hardly wait for Christmas and the chance to speak with Lexi's father. Being able to link the hand with music opened up a whole new source of possible grant money, and he intended to make the most of it.

Where was she? he wondered, just as the door opened.

"Hi." She stood and gestured him inside. "I'd just about given up on you."

She was wearing her hair down. He liked it down. "It took longer to pack up everything I needed than I thought." He stepped inside, but there wasn't much light. It was a smallish house, with cushy furniture and fluffy pillows. Candles were burning, making it smell sweet. A woman's house. "Where do you want me to set this up?"

"The piano is in here."

He followed her, noticing her walk for the first time. There was an interesting sway to it. He hadn't noticed the way she walked before. Maybe it was because she was wearing some black jumpsuit outfit.

He looked up just as she turned. "There aren't any tables, but I've got folding chairs you could set the laptop on. Will that help?"

"Sure." His arms were beginning to ache. As soon as they finished writing the documentation on the modifications they'd made in the last week and a half, he was going to have to get back to the gym.

Lexi left the room and returned with two folding chairs. When she bent over to open them, the pants stretched tight across her rear, revealing some interesting bumps.

Spencer smiled to himself. Probably little bows on her underwear. She looked like a ribbons-and-lace sort of woman. He wouldn't mind knowing for sure, though.

"Do you need another chair?" She frowned at the armload he carried. "I didn't realize there'd be so much equipment."

"Two chairs are fine, but I'll need an electrical outlet," he said. "And could you turn on more light?"

She hesitated, then walked over to the wall switch and flipped it.

"That's better." Spencer carefully set his laptop and the case containing the hand prototype on one of the chairs and sat on the floor. He flipped open the case and carefully removed the hand or, more accurately, the jumble of wires, electrical components and tiny motors that would one day be a hand.

"Have you had a chance to eat anything?" Lexi asked. "I can heat up something for you. Francesca and I get all sorts of wonderful goodies from the Wainright kitchen."

"Thanks, but I ate a sandwich from the vending machine right before I came over."

"Oh."

Spencer was busy hooking up the hand to a monitor, but his subconscious heard something in that "oh" that alerted him. He looked up at her, standing in the doorway, arms crossed over her chest.

Maybe Francesca had overstated Lexi's eagerness to fill in for her. "I really appreciate you taking the time to help me," he said.

"No problem."

Problem. But he didn't know what it was.

"Since you're not hungry, would you like something to drink?"

"A soft drink would be great."

Spencer concentrated on getting everything hooked up and was barely aware of Lexi's return. She knelt on the floor and tried to hand him a glass. He couldn't take it right then.

"Can you put it under the chair?"

"Sure."

When she leaned over to set the drink on the floor, he caught a whiff of her perfume. The candle scent had covered it up before. He liked her perfume and adjusted his position so he was just a little bit closer to her.

"How am I going to help you test the hand?" she asked.

"I'm mainly interested to see if you can use it at all, and the force you'll expend as you play the piano. I don't even know if this will be appropriate for pianists." He gave her a brief smile. "I've only got the thumb and index finger reconfigured, but we've got to start somewhere."

"Oh, I agree. There's a lot you can do with a thumb and an index finger."

He glanced at her, but she only smiled. She looked different somehow. "I'm going to have to hook electrodes up to you."

"Where?"

"Your head, arm and on your chest as a control."

"You're going to control my chest?"

Spencer nearly pinched himself with an alligator clip. "Just monitoring your heart rate."

"What for?"

"Your heart rate will increase under stress. It helps gauge the mental effort you have to expend to work the interface." He handed her a piece of sandpaper. "You can get started preparing your skin."

"Excuse me?"

She looked so taken aback that he laughed. "You have to rough up the surface of your skin for the electrodes. After you do that, I'll put this conducting medium on and stick the electrode over it."

"Lovely. Where exactly do I...?" She gestured.

Spencer put down the hand. "Here on your forearm. I can get seven kinds of feedback from the tendons here. Also on your temple." He touched his fingers to the side of her head. "The stuff is pretty greasy. It'll get in your hair. Sorry."

"It'll wash. And where on my chest?"

He looked down. "Right, uh…" There was a big zipper running down the length of her outfit.

He touched the area over his own heart.

"You mean here?" As if in slow motion, she pulled the zipper down several more inches.

Spencer stared as the metal track parted, hearing each tooth of the zipper separate, staring as more and more of her white skin came into view.

She pulled the collar to one side, and he could see the top of her bra. It was black, not pink and lacy like he'd thought.

No. Wrong. He wasn't supposed to notice her bra. This was science and he was a doctor. Not that kind of a doctor, but for tonight he would consider himself bound by the ethics of the profession.

And then she drew her fingers across the top swell of her breast and his mouth went dry. "Here?"

He swallowed. "Over a little more. And maybe down."

She moved her hand.

"No—"

"Show me." Blue eyes gazed into his.

Science, Spence. Science. Careful to touch only her fingers he positioned them where he wanted the electrode.

Abruptly he turned back to the hand. His own were sweating. He wiped them on his jeans. If he wasn't careful, he'd electrocute himself.

Lexi rubbed her skin with the sandpaper, and Spencer could hardly bear the thought of marring its smooth perfection.

He made mistakes hooking the hand up to the computer. Careless mistakes because he was trying to watch Lexi out of the corner of his eye so she wouldn't know it.

"I'm finished with this, I think." She held out her arm to show him, turned her head and pulled aside her collar. "Shall I go sit at the piano?"

"Yes."

Spencer brought the hand and its pulley system over to her. "First, I just want you to set your own hand over it. Play as normally as you can, and I'll take pressure readings." He attached the fingers to hers with tie wraps.

"This is not going to help my technique," she murmured. "It's heavy."

"You aren't auditioning for Carnegie Hall. Just do the best that you can." Spencer sat on the floor in front of the laptop. "Remember, only the thumb and first finger have the pressure grid working."

"Okay." She looked at him, waiting.

It must be the light, or something. Or maybe the angle. Spencer was sitting on the floor looking up at her, and it hit him all at once that Lexi Jordan was a beautiful woman. Her hair…the way she held herself…her expression… It wasn't any one element, but together… Wow!

From the first, he'd thought she was good-looking. Since their pool night, he'd found her attractive. And now…

And now he'd better concentrate on the reason he was here, though that was becoming incredibly difficult. "Anytime," he said.

Lexi nodded and started playing. It was music that started soft, then gradually got louder until he had a whole range of readings. But even though he was concentrating on the monitor, he was aware of the seductive melodies coming from the piano. The notes seemed to curl around him and tug him closer to her.

Lexi's music called to him, and he wanted to answer.

He shook his head, trying to clear it. They must be putting too many preservatives in the vending machine food. He was going to have to start brown-bagging it.

"That was perfect!" he said when she finished, trying to sound hearty to counter the effect of her music. It didn't work. "What was it?"

"Rachmaninoff." She used the mechanical hand to push her hair back from her face. "Did you like it?"

Like? His breathing was shallow. His heart rate had increased. He wanted to join with her in incandescent harmonies that would melt the piano keys. "Yes." He was still caught in the spell, unable to move.

After several motionless moments, she gave him a tiny smile that released him. "Good."

That the spell was now broken was a relief and a disappointment, but it was for the best. Starting something serious with Lexi and then approaching her father's foundation for a grant might cause complications. Exhaling, he stared at the tangle of wires on the floor next to him. "I think we're ready to attach the electrodes."

He dragged everything over to the piano. Sitting on the bench next to her, he dipped a cotton swab into the conductive jelly and smeared it over the red places Lexi had made on her arm and temple.

Then there was the third spot.

Spencer felt almost queasy inside, exactly the way he felt when approaching any challenge in which he was the underdog. And the challenge here was to remain clinically detached while swabbing the top of Lexi's breast.

Never had he been so aware of what he was doing. He'd worked with women before and hadn't had this reaction....

But had he ever seen skin so... *Pure* was the only word he could think of to describe the untouched quality it had. Soft and white, with curves in interesting places, the exposed triangle of Lexi's chest was about as far from the world of cold, metallic electrical components as he could get.

He drew another breath, hoping to clear his head, and only succeeded in drawing in the deep musky notes of her perfume.

What would happen if, instead of attaching the electrode, he just lowered his mouth and thoroughly kissed her?

LEATHER UNDERWEAR. Had she gone mad? She had no business wearing leather underwear. Leather was for lingerie professionals, like Francesca. Lexi was a white cotton amateur.

How embarrassing *could* this situation get? She'd unzipped herself practically to her navel. He *had* to have seen what she was wearing.

No reaction. None. Nothing.

Just look at the intent way those brown eyes were concentrating on all the electrical wires.

It was her own fault. All by herself she'd blown a stolen poinsettia and a platonic kiss, tongue or no tongue, all out of proportion. Then she'd compounded her error by listening to Francesca. And now she was suffering for it by sitting here in hardware-adorned leather underwear that was shouting, "Hey, stud, let's have a hot time tonight," and she couldn't shut it up.

She should have changed as soon as she realized that all he wanted to turn on were the lights.

"Ouch."

"Did I hurt you?" He was moving too fast, trying to remain professionally detached. Forget it. He wasn't professionally anything anymore.

"No, my hair caught on the zipper." She reached to untangle it.

"Try using the hand." He'd repositioned it so Lexi's own hand was in a fist and showed her how to use her knuckles to operate the two fingers that were functional.

After a few efforts, she clamped on the lock of hair. "I can feel that I'm holding something!"

"Does it feel like hair?"

"Sort of. I don't know whether I'd recognize it as hair, because I already know what I'm touching." She pulled, but her hair was really caught. "Oh," she said, and looked down at herself.

Spencer automatically looked down, too...then wished he hadn't. "What is it caught on?"

Lexi looked up at him with a funny expression. "Francesca's Christmas present."

"What?"

Her face colored. "It's...it's kind of a gag gift. And Francesca's going to order a set for herself—in red— but not if they're uncomfortable. And because they aren't returnable I'm wearing mine to test them for her," she finished in a rush.

"Wearing your what?"

"My, uh…I thought you noticed."

He'd noticed a lot, but he didn't know what was politic for him to admit to noticing. "The…the outfit?"

"Yes." She unzipped herself and pulled the edges of her top apart. "The leather."

Spencer stared at something that looked like it would have been worn by an Amazon warrior in a fantasy comic book. *That,* he hadn't noticed.

That, he hadn't expected.

That, he couldn't ignore.

"My hair is caught on one of the chains and I can't make this thing—" she waved the robotic hand "—work well enough to get it free. Could you…?"

Could he what? Continue to function while in the quivering throes of testosterone-induced shock? "Sure."

Between the hand, the chains and Lexi's unsuccessful attempts to free it, her hair was snarled pretty good.

First he untangled the hand.

That left the chain on the bra. It was a short chain with tiny links that lay flat against the leather. Trying very hard to avoid touching her more than necessary, Spencer nevertheless grazed his knuckles against her skin.

One of them gasped softly. He may have; she may have. It didn't really matter. All Spencer knew was that he could no longer remain in this unintended intimacy without doing something that involved skin, leather and his lips.

But her hair wasn't coming loose. In desperation, he tugged, and the chain gave.

The silver studs decorating the cup of the bra turned out to be more than decoration. They were working snaps. And the chain had been attached to one of them. The leather parted, revealing a generous crescent of skin.

Lexi gasped and clutched at herself with both hands. Or three, as it happened. "Oh! It tingles."

"Damn right. Sorry." He inhaled and exhaled twice. "I didn't mean to do that."

"Swear, or open the 'Gate of Delight'?"

"The *Gate of Delight?*" His voice didn't sound right, but Lexi didn't seem to notice.

"That's what Francesca said it was called...you know, this feels really weird." With an odd expression on her face, she continued to touch herself and the various zippers and chains with the hand, driving Spencer pretty much insane with lust. "It's kind of tingly. I can tell the difference between my skin and the leather. My skin is warm...the zipper pull is cold...and I can feel a texture variation...."

He should be thrilled. The sensor grid was working. He ought to be studying the data and recording her movements. Instead, he'd completely lost all scientific objectivity and was hypnotically watching the movements of her real fingers interact with those of the robotic hand while trying to figure out a way he could interact with her, too.

She touched his arm with the hand. "Do you feel a buzz?"

"Oh, yeah."

"The hand is supposed to do that?"

"I'm not talking about the hand." He skimmed

his fingers over the smooth skin of her neck and jaw. "I'm talking about you." He couldn't have prevented himself from kissing her right then for all the grant money in the world.

It was probably not the best move, considering he'd kissed her once—no, twice already. But each kiss had been different. The first was a sizzling kiss of discovery. The second... Well, the second was supposed to have been a simple goodbye kiss that had ended up getting complicated.

This one... This one was lust, pure and simple.

Okay, impure and unsimple, but once her lips parted under his, he didn't care. She was incredibly sexy, she was warm, she was in his arms and...

He was falling for her.

Hard. But he'd have to get right back up, because Spencer Price wasn't ready to fall for anybody. He needed to focus all his time and energy on the robotic hand. Grant money, even new grants, wouldn't last forever. Someone else was bound to develop a similar idea, and then all their work would be commercially useless, unless they were the first to perfect it.

His team was counting on him. And there was a certain professor he owed. Spencer was too close to let anything distract him now.

But he *was* falling for Lexi.

Falling for her soft, mobile mouth, the silky hair and the exotic perfume. Falling for the way he felt when she was in his arms. Falling for the expressions in her eyes. Falling for the emotions she revealed when she was lost in her music. Falling for the black leather. Even falling for her pitiful pool playing.

This was not good.

He broke the kiss long before he was ready and told himself he should feel guilty. He wasn't surprised when he didn't.

"It's a good thing that electrode isn't hooked up to my heart, because the monitor would be off the scale about now," she said breathlessly.

He grinned and touched his forehead to hers. "I want you to know that I came here strictly to test the hand."

"Then let's test it." She drew it up to cup his face. "Feel the tingles?"

He did. "Probably vibrations from the motors."

"Wonderful possibilities," she said, echoing his thoughts.

Closing her eyes, she mirrored with her own hand the movements of the robotic one. "I can feel your skin and a slight roughness from your beard," she said, moving it over his face. "I can feel the warmth...."

"Lexi, do you have any idea of what you're doing to me? I can't—"

"Then don't." And she kissed him until his head spun.

Somewhere in the far reaches of his mind, he knew this wasn't a good idea. "Are you sure?" he asked, barely breaking the kiss to do so.

"I'm beyond sure."

Spencer turned his head and placed a kiss in the palm of her real hand, then playfully kissed one of the working fingers of the robotic hand.

The buzz against his lips had a painful sharpness to it and he jerked. "I just got zapped."

That meant something important, but he lost the thought when Lexi leaned close.

"Shall I kiss it and make it better?"

He drew her into his arms, tried to kiss her, but pulled back. "My lips are numb." He glared at the traitorous hand.

Lexi laughed. "While you're getting the feeling back, I'm going to conduct my own tests." Still laughing, she managed to use the hand to work open the buttons on his shirt.

After that, Spencer pretty much went on autopilot. With Lexi reporting on all the sensations she felt, they got all the buttons undone, explored a couple of zippers on Francesca's Christmas present, then Lexi, wearing the sexiest smile he'd ever seen, said, "The ultimate test," and unsnapped his jeans.

All the air left his lungs in a whoosh and he was about to suggest adjourning to the bedroom, or sofa, or someplace besides the piano bench, when Lexi looked startled. "I think I broke it."

"What?" he gasped, very certain that everything he needed was fully functioning.

"The hand. It's hard to move the fingers." She trailed it down his stomach. "Do you feel the tingles anymore?"

He threw back his head. "The tingles are incredible."

"How incredible?" She moved lower.

"Wonderfully, fabulously incredible."

"You need a new texture reading," she said with a mischievous smile.

And the hand clamped over him.

Spencer experienced an instant of absolute ecstasy

before the pressure increased and the tingles became painful needle pricks.

"Lexi," he gasped just as there was an electrical sizzle and a burning smell. Not good. Very bad. No doubt a painful sign from above.

"Spencer, something's wrong!"

No kidding.

Lexi pulled at the hand. "I can't get it off!"

Nobody was getting anything off at this point. "Stop pulling!" Spencer fumbled for the power supply and jerked the plug out of the wall.

Eyes wide, Lexi frantically asked, "What do I do?"

Spencer grimaced. "Can you get yourself unhooked from the hand?"

"I think so."

"That would be a good place to start."

AFTER EXTRICATING themselves from the smoking hand, a mortified Lexi had driven Spencer to Rocky Falls's only after-hours medical clinic.

Much later, she helped Spencer pack up the equipment.

"We will look back on this and laugh some day," he promised, gingerly getting into his car.

"Yeah, too bad you already sent that letter to *Texas Men.*"

He started to laugh, then winced. "On the bright side, we know there is a design problem with the hand."

Lexi was fairly certain there were other, less humiliating ways to detect design flaws. "And on the dull side?"

He looked at her, managing a half smile. "I've got

a lot of work to do between now and Christmas, so I won't be able to see you until then."

Like that was a big surprise. From his comments in the car, she'd been anticipating a variation of the "this isn't going to work" talk. And it hadn't so far. He was lucky to have escaped with his manhood intact.

Still, Lexi pretended this entire evening would just be one amusing anecdote in her dating history, and waved goodbye from her front steps.

Then she went straight to the kitchen, got out all the leftover peppermint cheesecake from the Wainright and dug in.

NATURALLY, Francesca called from Indiana for a report.

So Lexi told her everything, except about eating the cheesecake.

"Was it horribly humiliating?" Francesca asked.

"Not as humiliating as having my underwear set off the metal detector in the emergency clinic."

Lexi could hear choked laughter.

"Is he…will he…can he, uh—"

"No, he hasn't become Rocky Falls's only castrati tenor. His…pride was bruised and his underwear was scorched. That's all."

"What a relief. Ah…"

"What?" Lexi grumbled.

"Well, does he have a lot to be proud of?"

Lexi sighed for lost opportunities. "I think so, but I only know thirdhand, so to speak."

Francesca chortled. "Lexi, you are so bad."

She groaned. "Not bad enough."

"So now what?" Francesca asked.

"Well, the hand's design needs tweaking."

"You two need tweaking." Her disgust sounded clearly over the phone.

"Uh, there is to be no tweaking until after Christmas. Doctor's orders." And she was certain *she* wouldn't be the tweaker.

"So what? You gave him a rain check?"

Lexi picked up the phone and walked across the hall from her bedroom until she could see Spencer's calendar picture still hanging in the bathroom. "After this little setback, not to mention spending Christmas with my family, do you honestly think that he'll want anything more to do with me?"

8

SPENCER FULLY RECOVERED, in spite of the fact that he couldn't stop thinking about Lexi. He'd never had trouble concentrating on his work before. Never. But then, he'd never met anyone like Lexi before.

And it didn't help that Rip had gone all metaphysical on him, lecturing about personal journeys and souls who traveled with a person. This from a man who took naps in a cave made of boxes.

Late one evening, when everyone had gone to dinner and Rip hadn't yet made his appearance, Spencer finally gave up and called her. There was no answer. When he checked with the Wainright Inn and discovered that Lexi was playing each night through the twenty-third, he rationalized that she was as busy as he was.

But that still didn't make it easier to concentrate.

BY DECEMBER twenty-third, Lexi's mother was calling her almost hourly, so she decided to spend the night at her parents' on Christmas Eve.

The imposing traditional white Colonial house, with a magnificent view of the falls, was not her childhood home. They'd lived in Kansas City, Fort Worth and finally, Austin, about an hour's drive away. But during Rocky Falls's development as a fine arts center, and the resulting building boom,

Lexi's parents had realized that it would soon be fashionable for wealthy Texans to have a vacation and retirement home here. The Cultural Arts Foundation agreed and built the house with an eye toward entertaining potential donors during their leisure time, as well as housing visiting guest artists. The Jordans would live there as long as her father was the chief trustee.

The only other time Lexi had stayed there was when she'd first come to Littletree and was looking for a roommate. It was not a kick-your-shoes-off kind of place, but Lexi figured she could keep her shoes on for a couple of days.

She arrived about threeish in the afternoon, and parked in the circular driveway right behind the delivery van from Main Street Drugs. Removing the garment bag and duffel containing her clothes and presents, she closed the door just as the delivery driver jogged down the front steps.

"Merry Christmas!" Lexi called.

The driver opened the door and tossed his clipboard inside. "Good luck."

Good luck?

Lexi climbed the steps. As soon as she raised her hand to ring the doorbell, she heard shouting.

"Catherine, I'm begging you. Take a tranquilizer!"

"*Drugs?* You want to drug me for Christmas?"

"Yes!"

Lexi rang the doorbell, then reached under the wreath and rapped the knocker for good measure.

There was an immediate cessation of hostilities, and her smiling parents opened the door to greet her.

Lexi was hit by the overwhelming scent of pine from the miles of garland draped everywhere. Lights twinkled. Gold glittered. A fire crackled. Christmas dripped throughout the foyer.

"Alexaaaandra." Her mother, wearing a white apron with an appliquéd Christmas tree on the bib, drew her inside. "Merry, merry Christmas, darling!" Her eyes were bright, and there was a hectic flush to her cheeks.

Her father wore a red sweater and a forest-green tie with Santa Claus faces on it. All he needed was a pipe.

The house looked like a movie set. Though Lexi had spent several afternoons decorating, her mother had worked untold hours turning the place into a Christmas fantasy.

"Merry Christmas, Mom and Dad. You look very homey. And the house is gorgeous, Mom."

Her mother beamed.

"Am I the first one here?" Lexi asked as her father took her garment bag and duffel.

"Yes. Leslie's plane arrives at six-thirty, which means dinner won't be until after eight."

Typical of her brother to schedule his flight for maximum inconvenience. "How about everyone else?"

Her mother's lips drew into a thin, martyrlike line. "Gretchen's therapist wishes to spend Christmas Eve with her own family, but it seems your sister can't bear to interact with us without her therapist."

"You don't mean she's not coming!" Lexi mentally calculated how long it would take to drive to Austin and drag her sister back by the hair.

Silently Lawrence threw up his hands and looked skyward.

"They're having a session together right now," Lexi's mother said, acting as if Gretchen's behavior was nothing out of the ordinary. Which it wasn't. "Dr. Tracey feels, and I have to agree with her, that Gretchen needs to have the entire Christmas experience, which means going to sleep anticipating the arrival of Santa Claus, and running eagerly down the stairs the next morning to see what new gifts are under the tree."

"We did that!" Lexi protested.

"Not after you and your brother enlightened her about Santa Claus."

"She's twenty-three. She's had years to get over it."

"Apparently she still harbors some resentment."

Lexi wasn't going to apologize. Besides, Les was the culprit, and only because Gretchen had told him that Santa liked her best.

She reached for her duffel. "Since I'm *not* Santa Claus, I can put my presents under the tree."

She unzipped the bag and started to withdraw her gifts, when her mother shook her head. "Oh, no, dear. You'll have to rewrap them in a coordinating paper. Gold, red, cream and forest-green only. Those are our Christmas colors. I thought it would be best to keep things very traditional."

"Well, I thought purple and hot pink looked rather zingy."

Her mother gripped her arm and closed her eyes. "Do not argue with me, Alexandra. Not at this happy time."

"I wasn't arguing, I just said—ouch!" She pulled

away from her mother's tightening grip and rubbed her arm.

"The paper is in my workroom upstairs."

Behind Catherine, Lexi's father held up a plastic bottle of prescription pills, and shook his head. Obviously her mother was unusually frazzled and it would be best to go along with whatever she wanted.

"Okay. I'll rewrap them."

Smile back in place once more, her mother opened her eyes. "Please make sharp creases on the corners."

If Lexi were her father, she'd grind up one of those little pills and give it to her mother in some eggnog. "Sharp creases. I'll remember."

Lexi's father started to carry her things up the stairs to the bedrooms. "Wait, Lawrence!"

Dutifully, he stopped.

"Alexandra, what did you bring to wear tomorrow?" Without waiting for a response, Catherine unzipped the garment bag, talking all the while. "You don't have to worry about pajamas. I bought the three of you matching pajamas in a darling red plaid that will look splendid in the photographs." She stared at Lexi's dress. "Blue? You brought blue denim to wear? This is *Christmas!*"

Lexi mentally ran through her wardrobe of dressy clothes. Mostly black, which was what she wore for performances. "I have a burgundy jacket—"

Catherine winced. "It will clash."

"Then I've only got black."

"Black isn't one of the colors. Black is not Christmas! And you can't wear stark white, either. We've got a cream and gold tablecloth. If you wear white, you'll make everything look dirty."

"Well, I—"

"Go shopping. Buy a new dress."

"Go shopping on Christmas Eve? No way."

Catherine turned to her husband. "Lawrence, give her a credit card."

Lexi's father reached for his wallet.

Okay, then. "Well, since you asked so nicely..." Lexi took the card, already glad of a chance to escape. Her poor father. She sent him a sympathetic look. "Is there anything I can pick up for you as long as I'll be out?"

"Rum."

"Lawrence!"

"For the eggnog, Catherine," he said mildly.

"What happened to the rum we had?"

Lawrence managed to look innocent. "There doesn't appear to be as much as I thought."

"Perhaps you'd better check the brandy supply, as well. We want enough to flame the plum pudding."

"Excellent suggestion." With a much lighter step, Lexi's father went off to check the bar.

Lexi made a mental note to buy brandy, as well.

"A nutmeg grater," her mother said, the idea seeming to come out of nowhere.

"A what?"

"I need a nutmeg grater. We have to have fresh nutmeg to sprinkle on the eggnog, and I had no idea it came in the form of these big...nuts." Her mother put her hands to her temples. "There are probably other things.... Lawrence! I'm giving Alexandra your cell phone!" Catherine opened the drawer in the hall credenza and withdrew the phone.

Oh, great. "Mom, it'll be so crowded and noisy, I might not hear it ring." But one look at her wild-eyed mother, and Lexi held out her hand.

Seconds later, a shrieking pierced the silence. At the same time, Lexi noticed another smell warring with the pine scent. Smoke.

Lawrence called from the back of the house. "Catherine! The smoke alarm in the kitchen is going off!"

"My cookies!" Lexi's mother ran down the hall.

"Bye, Mom!" Lexi called, and quickly let herself out the door.

GRETCHEN AND LES rolled in about the same time later that evening. Lexi couldn't help wishing they'd roll back out again.

If Christmas Eve dinner was a preview of tomorrow's main event, then Lexi was going to send Spencer away, always assuming he actually showed up. Being around her was proving hazardous to his health.

Upon her arrival, Gretchen had announced that she would not interact with the family until her therapist got there, then had gone up the stairs to her room.

Lexi didn't *want* to interact with Les. He'd arrived unshaven, greasy-headed, in ratty, paint-spattered clothes and wearing more earrings than Lexi owned. After hearing that Lexi was bringing Spencer, Les complained about missing "Arnaud." But no one cared about "Arnaud" after Les took off his jacket.

He wore a tank undershirt that showed off his tattoos. "I am an artist," he announced. "And the skin is my palette."

At that point, Catherine had cited the long day tomorrow, and had retired to bed. Lexi washed the dishes while Les and her father argued.

At six o'clock on Christmas morning, Lexi, attired in a ruffled plaid-flannel granny gown that would have given Francesca hives, woke up her brother and sister, made sure they put on their official Christmas pajamas, threatened them if they didn't behave, and herded them downstairs, stomping on the steps to alert their parents.

Just like old times.

Santa Claus had very cleverly brought them bicycles. Really good ones, too. Good enough to surprise delighted reactions from Gretchen and Les, which their father dutifully recorded with the video camera.

Because everyone was warming up to each other, because the house looked so pretty, because wonderful smells were coming from the kitchen and probably because their father had put champagne in the orange juice, Lexi could forgive herself for relaxing and thinking the day would go well.

Yesterday afternoon, against all odds, she'd found a soft cream wool dress that had a detachable vest embroidered with holly. After Christmas, she could take off the vest and wear the dress when she played at the Wainright Inn.

Even Emily's imminent arrival didn't bother her anymore, since Lexi's dear, sweet mother had brilliantly suggested that she invite a man, which is how Lexi found Spencer, whom she would be seeing in a few hours.

So all in all, she was in a good mood.

The good mood lasted until just outside the kitchen door.

"Then call her therapist!"

"Catherine, it's Christmas. We can't drag the woman away from her family at Christmas."

"Why not? This whole thing was her idea. A lot of good it's going to do if Gretchen won't come out of her room."

"She'll charge a fortune!"

"Is money more important to you than your daughter?"

"If you'd seen Dr. Tracey's last bill, you wouldn't ask that question."

Lexi walked into the kitchen. Putting on an apron covered with reindeer heads, she said, "Ignore Gretchen and she'll come out. After all, she can't be the center of attention if nobody knows she's here."

"Alexandra! Lawrence, call Dr. Tracey."

Sighing heavily, Lexi's father picked up the telephone, listened a moment, then quietly replaced it. "Gretchen already has. She was giving the woman directions on how to get here."

"Good. Now, when Dr. Tracey arrives, we'll just say she's Gretchen's friend."

"Catherine…"

His wife leveled a quelling look at him. "I don't wish my sister and her family to know that it is necessary for one of my children to have a therapist hold her hand so she can endure Christmas with us!"

Lawrence surrendered. "Okay. Whatever you want."

"Hey, Dad, is the eggnog ready yet?" Lexi asked brightly, still determined to salvage her good mood.

"Don't give her any, Lawrence. She'll spoil her appetite."

He gave Lexi a sympathetic look. "I was just getting ready to make it."

"Lawrence, before you mix the eggnog, make sure there's enough wood so the fire will last the day. That might be a good project for Leslie."

"Leslie is riding his new bike."

"Now there's a blast from the past," Lexi said. "Anything to avoid chores."

"Alexandra! I'm sure Leslie will see to the wood, if he's asked nicely instead of badgered." Lexi's mother raised her eyebrows and Lawrence headed out the kitchen.

As he walked past Lexi, he leaned down and whispered, "There's more special orange juice in the fridge."

"Thanks, Dad. How have you stood it the last couple of weeks?"

He smiled down at her. "This dinner is important to your mother. She's trying to prove something—either to herself, to her sister, to you kids, I don't know, but the best thing we can do is support her. It'll all be over soon, and things will be back to normal."

"When they *are* back to normal," Lexi said, drawing a breath, "I'd like to speak with you. It's about the music building at Littletree."

Her father raised his eyebrows. "What about it?"

Lexi smiled. "I'll tell you later."

"I'll be holed up in the den," her father said and quietly slipped out.

A few minutes later the doorbell rang and Catherine yelped. "It's only ten forty-five! That better not be my sister!"

But of course it was.

Lexi followed her mother to the front door where her aunt and uncle were just being greeted by her father.

"Ben! Carolyn!" Lexi's mother appeared truly delighted.

What an actress, Lexi thought, looking behind her aunt and uncle for signs of her cousin. Nothing.

"Ben, I'm making eggnog and need your opinion." Lexi's father neatly rescued her uncle.

"I thought we'd come early to help," Aunt Carolyn said as soon as she entered. She swept an assessing gaze around the pine-bedecked foyer and banisters, but made no comment.

"That's kind of you, but there's really hardly anything left to do." Lexi's mother hung up their coats in the front closet. "I've got everything under control."

Lexi hoped that was true, since she hadn't been in the kitchen long enough to see the true status of Christmas dinner.

Carolyn appeared delighted. "How wonderful. I must confess, I had my doubts, Catherine, since you'd never had the entire family for Christmas, and big gatherings can be so stressful."

"I frequently entertain on an even larger scale." There was an edge to Catherine's voice.

"*Do* you? And here I thought entertaining intimidated you."

Lexi drew in her breath, but was too late to save her mother from falling into the trap.

"Oh, no. I love giving parties."

"Since I've never been invited, I had no idea."

Catherine patted her sister's arm. "But most are entertainments for the foundation donors. You understand."

"So you're saying I have to purchase an invitation to one of your parties?"

"Where's Emily?" Lexi broke in, using the bright, chirpy voice that was becoming her standard today.

"She's just a few minutes behind us," Aunt Carolyn answered. "I'll wait by the door so I can open it as soon as she gets here. She mustn't take chances with her throat by standing in the cold. Speaking of...." Carolyn rubbed her arms. "Could you scoot the furnace up just another notch, or two? These big places can be so drafty."

"We have a blazing fire in the fireplace," Lexi's mother said tightly. "Emily can sit near it if she's cold."

"But what about when we eat? Do you have a fireplace in the dining room, too?"

"No, but—"

"There are responsibilities when you entertain great talent, Catherine."

"I will have you know that some of the world's top artists and musicians have stayed in this house, and I've never had any complaints," Lexi's mother said huffily.

"Yes, but have they ever returned?"

"Mom, didn't you leave something cooking on the stove?" Lexi stepped between them and urged her mother toward the kitchen.

"Oh, I hope it's not the gravy," Carolyn said. "I can't abide lumpy gravy."

"I wouldn't have known that from eating yours!"

"I'll turn up the heat, Aunt Carolyn," Lexi shouted over her mother.

The thermostat was in the hall leading to the utility room, and Lexi turned it up a couple of notches as they went past.

"The temperature is perfectly fine in here, and she knows it! And once everyone is seated in the dining room, it'll be stifling."

Her mother was right. It was a typically mild winter day that would heat up later in the afternoon. At least the weather was clear, so there was no chance of anyone being stranded in a freak snowstorm, Lexi thought.

"Okay, Mom. Let's get this show on the road. What shall I…" Lexi had been looking around the kitchen as she spoke. There were dirty dishes in the sink, a stack of cookbooks, the chopping board and several trays on the counter… And the only thing cooking on the stove was the plum pudding rattling in its pudding steamer. The source of the wonderful smells appeared to be the oven, where Lexi could hear the goose sizzling.

"Uh, Mom?"

"Yes?" Catherine was at the refrigerator.

"You've got the goose in the oven. Shouldn't we start on the side dishes?"

Her mother fanned her flushed face. "Well, I was going to, but now that Carolyn is here, we'll have to make the appetizers."

"I can do that." They were hours away from eating. Not a good sign. "You concentrate on dinner."

"I have been concentrating on dinner! I didn't realize everything would take so long. Just making the stuffing took me an hour. The caterers don't take an hour to make stuffing."

"They've had more practice," Lexi soothed. *I will not panic. Mom is panicking enough for both of us.* "Now what have you planned for appetizers?"

What her mother had planned was a complicated dish featuring a crabmeat stuffing with phyllo dough wrapped around it and the ends twisted so the resulting pastry resembled a firecracker.

Oh, and no canned crabmeat for her mother. No, Lexi had to find a hammer and pound crab shells, then begin the tedious process of extricating enough crabmeat for the recipe. It would take forever.

While her mother was involved with grinding salmon in a blender, Lexi stole to the pantry where she knew her mother kept emergency supplies of crackers and cheese spread. Let Aunt Carolyn gnaw on those for a while.

Lexi was furtively carrying a tray of very ordinary cheese and crackers into the living room when the doorbell sounded. Aunt Carolyn yanked it open. Lexi's heart thudded heavily at the sight of the male silhouette, but it wasn't Spencer.

"Oh, good, you're here. Come in, Marshall."

"I want to make a quick check to see if everything is ready for Emily," he said.

Still wearing his coat, he followed Carolyn into the living room. Lexi followed him.

Marshall DeSalvo, Emily's husband, was older than Lexi remembered, but she hadn't seen him recently.

Maybe living with Emily had taken it out of him, she thought with a smirk.

While she'd been waiting, Lexi's aunt had rearranged the furniture so that a comfortable wing chair was facing the fireplace. Never mind that it destroyed the conversational grouping.

"Good. That will be acceptable." Marshall scanned the room like a Secret Service agent, then licked his finger and held it up while he walked in a circle. "Draft in the southeast quadrant," he said.

"I'll sit there," Carolyn said quickly.

Without acknowledging this bit of maternal sacrifice, Marshall walked toward Lexi and stared at the tray she still held. "No milk products. They clog the voice." He walked on.

"And your mother says she's entertained singers." Shaking her head, Carolyn followed her son-in-law.

"I guess eggnog's out, then." Lexi looked down at the tray and popped a cracker into her mouth. A clogged voice might keep her from saying something she regretted.

Lexi had just set the tray down when there was a commotion in the entryway.

"This way, darling."

"We've got you set up in here, Em."

"Daddy, I'm hungry."

"There's no video in here. You said we could watch our movie."

"You didn't bring that mermaid one, did you?"

"It's my favorite! Daddy said we could watch it!"

"Marshall, the children," said a pampered feminine voice.

"Derek, let your sister watch *The Little Mermaid*, then you can watch *Mutant Martian Ninjas Attack Seattle*."

Lexi backed up just as a crowd of people clothed in velvet, lace and red plaid, boiled into the room.

At the center, scarf wrapped around her throat, was a dainty blonde dressed in celestial blue.

Emily DeSalvo and her entourage had arrived.

Fascinated, Lexi watched as Emily was arranged by the fire, with her pouting, but well-behaved children following in her wake.

"Hi, Emily," she said, walking over to her cousin.

Emily silently pressed her throat, but acknowledged Lexi with a regal nod.

Aunt Carolyn handed her Emily's scarf.

Marshall handed her a silver thermos with Emily's monogram. "This is Emily's special vitamin drink. It should be served warm."

"Thanks, but I don't think there's enough here for everybody," Lexi said.

Marshall only blinked.

"Kidding. I'll just..." She motioned toward the kitchen as she backed away.

She was passing through the entryway just as a shadow appeared at the door. Not tall enough for Spencer, Lexi thought as the bell rang.

A woman with hair as black as her own stood here. "I'm Dr. Tracey, here for Gretchen Jordan."

"Come in," Lexi said. "I'm her sister, Lexi. You should know that we're telling people you're her friend."

"Of course I'm her friend—in a professional capacity."

"Dr. Traceeeeeeey!"

The last syllable of the doctor's name became a scream as Gretchen launched herself down the stairs. "I can't do it without you!"

There was a sudden silence from the living room.

Dr. Tracey moved to the stairs and ushered Gretchen back up them. "Gretchen, have you been in your room all morning?"

"I tried, I really tried." Gretchen began to sob.

"Do you want to talk about it?"

"Lexi got more presents than I did!"

"And how did that make you feel?"

"Excuse me," Lexi called after them. "So what if I got an extra pair of socks? You got diamond ear studs!"

Becoming aware of her audience, Lexi turned and smiled, showing lots of teeth. "I'll go see how dinner's coming."

As she passed the door to the den, she heard the faint sounds of the football game her father and Uncle Ben were watching. That would soon be replaced by *The Little Mermaid*, Lexi bet.

The instant Lexi walked into the kitchen, she knew something was wrong. A strong burnt electrical smell hung in the air. The last time she'd smelled burnt wiring had ended with an embarrassing trip to the Rocky Falls after-hours emergency clinic.

Lexi's mother was trying to counter the odor with cinnamon spray potpourri. "I fried the blender," she said, visibly fighting for calm. "We were supposed to have salmon mousse for the first course."

"So the mousse will be a little chunky."

"But it's supposed to set for four hours. I don't have four hours."

"Then pour it into bowls and call it salmon soup."

"Do you think they'll know?"

Lexi shook her head.

Catherine relaxed. "You'll have to reset the table. I didn't put out bowls."

"Not a problem."

The next two hours raced by before Lexi could begin to worry if Spencer would show up, or if she even wanted him to.

Things were not going well.

At Dr. Tracey's urging, Gretchen came into the kitchen so she could fully experience Christmas, but she was more trouble than help. Lexi finally let Gretchen sit at the table and decorate sugar cookies while Dr. Tracey discussed the meaning of her color choices with her.

Their mother had planned a far too ambitious menu, especially for someone who wasn't used to cooking. Throughout, a blue haze hung in the air because the fat from the roasting goose splattered and burned the inside of the oven.

Aunt Carolyn periodically drifted back to complain that the "heavy air" couldn't be good for Emily's throat, and was shooed away.

And it wasn't that they were ever unaware of the goose. It was that they'd become desensitized to the burning smell, and they'd turned off the smoke alarm.

"Catherine, darling?" Lexi's father ventured to stick his head in the kitchen. "Is everything quite all right?"

"Quite."

"Then you intend to have smoke pouring out the oven vents?"

"It's just a little grease from the—" She gasped. Smoke rolled out the oven vents where it collected in a blue cloud near the ceiling and drifted toward the exhaust fans.

Lexi's mother whimpered as she jerked open the oven and was enveloped in a cloud of smoke. It was several minutes before they could see inside to remove the goose. Catherine took one look and staggered backward, clutching her heart.

It was left to Lexi to reach in and remove the shrunken, blackened carcass.

"It is not your failure. It is the goose's failure," intoned Dr. Tracey, already by Catherine's side.

Lexi noticed the change in pitch from the rattling pudding steamer an instant before the others. "Mom, the steamer doesn't sound—"

With a loud retort, the lid to the pudding steamer blew off with such force that it hit the ceiling, sprinkling pieces of plaster over the range and into the salmon mousse soup. Then the lid landed in the soup, splashing it over the counter and floor.

Catherine moaned. "What am I going to do? What am I going to do?" she repeated over and over again.

"Uh, hello in there?" It was Uncle Ben. "I've got a young man here who says he's come for Christmas dinner."

Through the haze, looking like the white knight he was, stood Spencer Price.

And in his arms was a smoked turkey.

9

WHEN SPENCER DROVE UP to Lexi's parents' home, he'd very nearly kept going right around the circular driveway, but he'd given his word he'd be here.

Besides, after trying to avoid thinking of her for days he was ready to see her again. More than ready.

And then he'd seen her house. Normally, wealth no longer intimidated him. Constantly canvassing for money for his projects among the politically and corporately powerful had desensitized him.

It had been a long time since his background had betrayed him, but he couldn't help being a little intimidated by this place. It screamed money. He was surprised the wreath on the front door wasn't made of dollar bills.

He mentally compared it to the humble ranch-style house outside Dallas where he'd spent the night. He hadn't lived with Ma and Pa McKinney the longest, but they'd been his last set of foster parents, the ones who'd helped him fill out the forms for boarding school, and he considered their place as close to a home as he had.

It was just the comparison to this house, he thought, shaking off his momentary reservations. Although he did wish Lexi hadn't talked him into bringing a turkey.

Too late now. Fortunately, he'd also brought a bottle of port from a Texas winery he enjoyed introducing people to.

He got out of the car, opened the trunk and stared at the white foam ice chest. What were these people going to do with a smoked turkey? He almost left it in the car, but at the last moment, he pulled the plastic sack out of the cooler, grabbed the port and slammed the trunk before he could change his mind.

At the bottom of the steps, he smelled smoke. At that moment, the front door opened and a white-haired man he didn't recognize propped it back with a gold angel.

"Hello," Spencer said, climbing the steps. "I'm Spencer Price—a friend of Lex—uh, Alexandra's. She invited me for dinner."

The man straightened. "Well, I don't know about the dinner prospects, but Alexandra's dad makes a mean eggnog." He held out his hand when Spencer reached the top of the stairs. "I'm Ben Willman, her uncle."

Spencer had to transfer the turkey to his other hand in order to shake Lexi's uncle's. He sincerely hoped the man couldn't tell what was in the sack.

Through the open door, Spencer saw a house that looked like it had been decorated by Martha Stewart, except for the haze.

"I believe they're all back in the kitchen." Mr. Willman gestured for Spencer to follow him. "There's been some commotion."

The smoke became thicker, the closer Spencer got to the kitchen. He could hear Lexi's mother saying, "What am I going to do?" over and over.

Lexi's uncle stopped in the doorway. "Uh, hello in

there? I've got a young man who says he's come for Christmas dinner."

"Spencer!" Lexi's face glowed with such joy and relief that he was momentarily stopped by it. No wonder she'd stayed in his thoughts.

She set a blackened roasting pan on the kitchen butcher block island and walked over to him. "You're here!"

"Yes. Merry Christmas." He nodded to the charred lump in the pan. "Is that the goose?"

"It was, but we may have to call in the carbon-dating experts to make sure."

Spencer was stunned. She'd deliberately burned the goose so he'd look good with his turkey gift. That took guts.

She nodded to the sack he held. "Is that, I fervently hope, a smoked turkey?"

He nodded and opened the sack, thinking how close he'd come to not bringing a turkey at all.

Closing her eyes, she exhaled. "Thank you," she whispered. Turning, she said, "Mom, look what Spencer brought us. A smoked turkey! How about that?"

Mrs. Jordan stared, and tears filled her eyes. "Oh, Dr. Price, you've saved Christmas!"

"I wouldn't go that far." Spencer looked around the kitchen. "I'm sure you've got plenty of other…food." Some of which was dripping down the wall behind the stove.

"Mom, the turkey is fully cooked, so all we have to do is heat it. By the time it's hot, we'll have the rest of dinner ready to serve." Lexi was already unwrapping the bird, but her mother stopped her.

"It's so smoky in here. Why don't you show Spencer—may I call you Spencer?"

He nodded.

"Show Spencer the gardens until the smoke clears."

"But there's the, uh…" Lexi glanced toward the stove which her father had just turned off.

It was splattered with pink goo.

"Please." Her mother made shooing motions. "Lawrence, will you be a dear and freshen the stove?"

Lexi gestured to the back door. "Let's go this way. The backyard has a great view of the falls."

Avoiding splatters of pink on the floor, Spencer followed Lexi toward two dark-haired women who'd been decorating cookies.

At first Spencer thought she wasn't going to stop, but she did. "Spencer, this is my sister, Gretchen, and her friend—"

"Dr. Tracey is my therapist," interrupted Gretchen. She looked at Lexi. "I'm not ashamed of it. It's important, and I don't keep important secrets from family members." She turned her head away.

Beside him, Spencer felt Lexi tense.

The therapist looked at him. "Gretchen heard you addressed as Dr. Price."

"I'm an engineer," he explained.

She dismissed him with a flick of her eyes and turned back to Lexi's sister. "You see? Your family didn't bring in another doctor for you."

Still sullen, Gretchen glared at him, and Spencer got the distinct impression that she would have preferred that he'd been another therapist. This was one high-maintenance woman.

"Gretchen, the world doesn't revolve around *you*, you know," Lexi burst out.

Her comment didn't go over well with Dr. What's-her-name.

Or with the sister. "If he's not a doctor, then he's your boyfriend."

Lexi just looked at her.

"Gretchen is feeling excluded since you didn't confide in her," Dr. Tracey explained in a quietly professional voice, which Spencer knew was supposed to soothe, but he'd always found such a voice irritatingly patronizing.

"Confide what?" Lexi asked.

"About your boyfriend."

"We haven't been dating long," Spencer said.

"Long enough for you to come to our *family* Christmas dinner," Gretchen said accusingly. "Today is Christmas. It's supposed to be for *our* family."

"Just because you're in therapy doesn't mean you get to be rude!" Lexi told her. "Come on, Spencer."

"I'm only expressing my feelings."

"Gretchen," began Dr. Tracey.

"He doesn't belong here!" she said.

Lexi's sister couldn't possibly know his circumstances, but that didn't make the sting any less painful. "Your parents were very kind to invite me," Spencer said as evenly as he could. The woman was in therapy. She didn't need him to unload on her, but he couldn't resist adding, "You're very lucky that you have a family you can be with today. Some people don't."

He was conscious of Lexi's questioning look, but didn't meet her eyes. Instead, he headed out the back door before he said something that would set Gretchen off again.

"I'm sorry," Lexi said as soon as she caught up with him on the patio. "I swear, with Gretchen anything you say is going to be twisted and used against you."

He stared out at the falls. "Don't worry about it."

She was silent for a moment. "I think you've suffered at my hands enough. Gretchen obviously upset you, and you've more than fulfilled your part of our agreement. Go on home, have a Merry Christmas and I'll make up an excuse to tell my parents."

He was going to have to explain. He glanced at her, then back out at the falls. From this angle, he couldn't see the research building, but wished he could. It would be a comforting reminder of how far he'd come in his life. "I grew up in foster homes," he said abruptly.

"Did you?"

"I just said I did," he snapped.

"From the way you spoke, I couldn't tell what kind of a response you wanted from me."

"An honest one."

"Then, honestly, I wish you'd tell me about it. But in spite of the fact that *you* brought up the subject, you seem very touchy. Is that honest enough for you?"

"Maybe a little too honest," he grumbled.

She pointed back to the kitchen. "My family and all its foibles is on full and glorious display back there, but I don't know anything about yours."

"No father, mother an alcoholic, grandmother couldn't take me in. That's it."

He hadn't wanted sympathy, and he didn't get it. He got a toss of her head and an irritated look.

"You don't have to talk about it if you don't want to."

"I *am* talking about it! There's nothing more to say."

"There's plenty more to say, but I'm not going to dig it out of you. If you want to tell me, you'll tell me." She walked to the edge of the patio.

He stared after her. This wasn't the way the conversation was supposed to go. "Lexi?"

She looked back.

"I...don't tell people about it. There have been times when my background has worked against me." He managed a smile. "It's hard to know where to start."

"I think your experience would impress people," she said at last. "You obviously had to work very hard to get where you are."

The breeze picked up, lifting her hair and tossing it across her face. She tucked the strands behind her ears. "That's your cue to tell me how you *did* manage to become head of a research team."

He shrugged. "I didn't have that as my actual goal in life. All I wanted was a normal, stable environment. Don't get me wrong. I stayed with good people, but we all knew it was only temporary. Then I saw these old movies on television—the foreign ones where the men wore their school ties. It didn't matter what any of them did as adults, the others would support them because they'd gone to the same school. They lived there—all the time."

"That's boarding school."

He nodded. "I kept having to change schools because I was moved around so much, so I figured if I lived at the school, I might have some stability."

Lexi rubbed her arms. "That was really smart of you."

"Yeah, well a couple of things were against me." Spencer had been so caught up in what he'd been saying that he hadn't considered that Lexi had come outside in just a dress and apron.

He shrugged out of his fleece-lined jacket and put it over her shoulders. She snuggled into it and he knew that next time he wore it, he'd be able to smell faint traces of her perfume.

"First of all, I was in the wrong country, it wasn't the thirties and I didn't come from boarding school money. But I asked around, went to the library and eventually found out about prep schools. I wanted one where I could stay there year-round and get out of the foster system. A place that had uniforms so my clothes wouldn't stand out. I also knew that the only way I could get there was on a scholarship, or if someone sponsored me. So I studied like a maniac and polished my schmooze skills. Then I applied everywhere until this place in Pennsylvania offered me a scholarship."

"And you got there only to discover that they made fun of your background because you weren't 'one of them,' right?"

"Bingo."

Sympathy shone in her clear blue eyes, but before it could make him uncomfortable, she leaned over and pinched his cheek. "Well, it's a good thing you're a major cutie, or you wouldn't have had such an easy time of it."

"Hey, I'm spilling my guts here." But he grinned.

"I know. And I hope *you* know that no one here is going to act like those little cretins at your boarding school."

He hated to ask, but he had to know. "Isn't that why you burned the goose?"

"What are you talking about?"

"You told me to bring the turkey and then you burned the goose so I'd look good. You were afraid your parents were going to see through me."

She looked flabbergasted. "That is the most—Spencer, if anything, my parents should be worried that you'll see through *them*. That's not *their* money they give away."

"Then whose is it?"

"The Cultural Arts Foundation's. My father is just an employee." She flung her arm all around them. "The foundation owns all this. My parents don't dwell on that fact, though. I think that's why they wanted at least one of their children to be the performer Emily is—so they would have a legitimate entree to the arts world. And other than Emily, my aunt Carolyn doesn't care about the society aspects at all. It's like Emily and I were born into the wrong families."

She blinked at him, and he realized she'd just spilled *her* guts. He remembered her mother's scathing remarks about Lexi not using her talent and figured Lexi was remembering them, too.

He stared at her, feeling a strange bonding, one he'd never felt with a woman. She'd been hurt, too. It shone clearly in her eyes. Spencer didn't like seeing it there. He didn't know what to do, or say, so he fell back on one of his tried-and-true moves.

He kissed her.

Just reached out, pulled her to him and kissed her, reveling in the fact that he could hold her in his arms again.

And that was the exact instant her mother discovered them. "Alexandra?" she called from the French doors.

They jerked apart.

"Oh, you two." She beamed at them fondly. "And there isn't even any mistletoe out here."

They stood staring at each other, their breaths coming quickly, making little white puffs.

Spencer felt cold, and not because he was no longer wearing his jacket. Lexi knew why he was here, but being caught sneaking a kiss from the daughter of the house by her mother implied something else entirely, and it made him uneasy, as did the soft look in Lexi's eyes.

"Come inside at once." Mrs. Jordan beckoned. "I have the most wonderful news. Emily has agreed to sing for us before we eat!"

"Was there ever any doubt?" Lexi asked, shrugging out of Spencer's coat.

Her mother blinked. "You just don't assume a person of Emily's stature will sing at every occasion she attends. And, too, there was the smoke." She closed the doors after them. "Spencer, this will be such a treat for you."

"I'm looking forward to it," he said.

"And so you should. While Emily is warming up in the music room, we can present you to the others." Mrs. Jordan frowned. "You can't perform in an apron," she said to Lexi.

"I thought Emily was performing."

"Naturally she'll need an accompanist."

"And that would be me."

"Alexandra, don't be difficult. This is an honor."

An honor? An *honor?* Lexi untied the apron and pulled the bib over her head. "Mom, this is *Emily* you're talking about." But her mother and Spencer had walked on ahead.

Lexi stopped by the kitchen to hang the apron on a hook inside the pantry door, then headed toward the music room. Once she was in the hallway, she could hear Emily me-ma-maw-mo-mooing in the music room.

The music room was actually built specifically as a music room. Artists performing in nearby Austin, or even Houston or Dallas welcomed the retreatlike atmosphere of the big house in Rocky Falls when they stayed here, but they still had to practice. Occasionally, Lexi's parents, representing the foundation, would have musicales and receptions, so the room saw fairly frequent use.

Only Emily and Marshall were in the room now, with the others waiting outside until Emily was warmed up. Lexi closed the door behind her, but neither Emily nor her husband acknowledged her, so she walked across the wooden floor toward the piano. It was hard to creep across a wooden floor, but she needn't have bothered for all the response she got.

Marshall played a series of ever-higher chords as Emily's voice soared up and down the scale. Standing right beside the piano bench, Lexi waited until the warm-up exercise reached its natural conclusion.

"So what are we sing—"

Both Marshall and Emily held out their hands and launched into another exercise.

"Look, if you don't need me, just say so. I'm sure I can find something else to do." And someone to do it with.

Emily began a series of nasal humming sounds.

"Can't you see she's in the middle of warm-ups?" Marshall snapped. "As a professional, I assumed you'd know she couldn't be interrupted. But then again, Littletree isn't exactly Juilliard, is it?"

Lexi didn't like Marshall very much. She leveled a look at him. "She isn't the only one who needs to warm up. What does she want me to play for her?"

Emily continued humming as Marshall unzipped a leather portfolio. "Anticipating that Emily would be asked to 'sing for her supper,'" he said with a disparaging smile, "I brought a selection of seasonal music." He paged through it. "I don't think you need to use full voice, Emily. I'll pull a selection of lighter carols."

"You mean like 'Rudolph the Red-nosed Reindeer'?" Lexi asked.

Marshall didn't even look up.

"I'd like to sing 'O Holy Night,'" Emily said. "It has quite a nice accompaniment with it." She smiled at Lexi, and went back to humming, a finger in one ear.

She speaks! Lexi thought.

"Not today, Emily," Marshall said. "That'll require full voice, and there's no sense in taxing yourself. I'm not even sure I'll let you sing 'Silent Night.'"

Lexi looked at his graying temples and the black wire-rim glasses he wore. "Aren't you an accountant?'' she asked him. The fact that he was still sitting on the piano bench and she was still standing beside it made her cranky.

"I'm Emily's business manager, and in the absence of her vocal coach, I must look out for her resources, namely her voice." He spoke dispassionately.

Lexi stared first at him, then at Emily, who was still vocalizing. After meeting her eyes for a brief, but telling moment, Emily turned away.

How could she let this—this *accountant* bully her around? Emily should be able to sing whatever she wanted to.

So a family Christmas dinner wasn't important enough for "full voice," was it?

"Since Emily's resources are so limited, she shouldn't sing today at all. Don't worry about it for a moment." Lexi walked to the other side of the bench and sat, forcing Marshall to scoot to the edge. "I brought plenty of seasonal music, as well."

She put her hands on the keyboard and looked at him. "You're in the way."

A nonplussed Marshall stood, Lexi adjusted the bench, then launched into the Christmas medley she had been playing all month at the Wainright Inn.

That jerk, Marshall, made her angry. Even more, she pitied Emily. What kind of life did she have anyway? She was nothing more than a "resource" to her husband. *He* decided when and where and what she'd sing. How awful. Lexi never wanted a man to have that much power over her.

Spencer wouldn't be like that, she knew. He'd be too busy with his own projects to take over her life the way Marshall had taken over Emily's.

Lexi lost herself in the medley and was surprised to hear applause when she finished. At some point during her angry performance, everyone had filed in and was sitting in the special Wedgwood-blue velvet chairs.

"Thank you, Alexandra," her mother said. "And now Emily." She clasped her hands together. "This is going to be such a treat."

And they hadn't even had a chance to rehearse together. "Emily and I need a moment," Lexi said, and gestured for Emily to come to the piano.

When Emily looked at her husband as if for permission, Lexi gritted her teeth. "Bring the music," she called, hoping Emily would bring the whole portfolio, but no, she brought only the pieces Marshall had selected. For a world-famous opera star, she'd sure turned into a wimp.

"Is Mommy going to sing?" asked Melissa in a stage whisper.

"Apparently so," replied her father.

Lexi even felt sorry for the kids.

Emily reached the piano and handed Lexi the music.

"This is like old times, isn't it, Em?" Lexi paged through the music.

"Nothing is like old times," Emily said, but there was no self-pity in her voice.

Lexi would love to have a heart-to-heart with Emily—and tape it to play for her mother later—but doubted she'd get the chance. "So what are you singing?"

They settled on "Away in a Manger" for the children, "What Child is This?" and "Joy to the World."

Lexi began playing. Even though the melody and

accompaniment were simple, it was obvious from the first notes that the song was being sung by a master.

As she played the first carol, Lexi watched the faces of Emily's children and had a sudden realization: they didn't get to see their mother a lot. And this was the kind of life Lexi's mother had wanted for her?

The second carol didn't stretch Emily much, either. Still, Lexi could tell Emily was good. No, great. Far better than anyone on the vocal faculty at Littletree.

The thought depressed her. Greatness inspires greatness. Lexi found herself raising her own standard of playing. How long had it been since she'd stretched herself? And how would Littletree ever attract talent even half as good as Emily with the inadequate facilities there now? She was more determined than ever to appeal to her father.

It was time for the third carol they'd selected.

Lexi stared at the introduction, then at Emily, poised to begin singing a triumphant "Joy to the World." Honestly. So far, this little recital had been like test driving an Indy 500 race car around the block. They needed a quarter mile track to see what it could do.

They needed "O Holy Night."

And that's what Lexi began playing. Emily swallowed once, but didn't flinch and didn't shake her head.

She opened her mouth and sang. She sang in full and glorious voice with the clear soprano that had soared to the highest balconies of the greatest opera halls in the world.

And Lexi soared with her. Her mother had been right. It *was* an honor to play for Emily. But Lexi no longer envied her, neither did she pity her. Emily had made choices for her art, choices for which she'd paid a price.

A price, Lexi realized, she wouldn't have paid.

10

"Wow." Spencer was waiting for her as everyone crowded around Emily.

Even Dr. Tracey had momentarily forgotten Gretchen and was proving that she could be as starstruck as anyone. Les, who'd been standing against the back wall, had slipped out, his expression eerily close to Gretchen's sullen one.

"She's great, isn't she?" Lexi tucked her hair behind her ears.

"I was talking about you."

"Playing with her inspired me." Lexi looked across the music room to where the angelic Emily was holding court. "I used to be jealous, but I'm not anymore. However, I *am* determined to revitalize the Littletree music department." She gave him a wry smile. "All it takes is money."

"Raising money is something I'm very good at," Spencer said with a grin.

"Ah, yes, the calendar."

"Francesca already has her picture."

Lexi laughed and by unspoken agreement, they headed toward the door.

"We've washed cars, had bake sales—"

"You're the guys who had the dunking booth!" Lexi remembered.

"Guilty. Also Appliance Repair Day."

"Why all the gimmicks?"

"That's what I'm trying to tell you. They generate publicity and publicity leads to name recognition, which leads to money. Every time I was interviewed, I'd work in all the stats about the hand, how it could benefit society, and my sponsors. They love publicity. When it came time to apply for other grants, I'd enclose press clippings."

Lexi began to get ideas. "The music department could do that."

"Sure you could. I'll be glad to brainstorm with you."

"Okay. We'll have to get together after the holidays." *That's a test, Spencer.* After the kiss on the patio, she needed to test him. That was no lust kiss, that was a you-mean-something-to-me kiss. It was a kiss that gave a girl hope that she hadn't blown it with a malfunctioning robotic hand.

She waited to see what he'd say, and when he only nodded, she felt a warm satisfaction spread through her.

Incredibly, wonderfully and impossibly, it appeared that Mr. December might become Mr. January, and who knows? Maybe she and Francesca wouldn't have to exchange black roses on Valentine's Day.

"Have we got a few minutes before we eat?" he asked.

"Probably more than a few," Lexi said.

"I've got a present for you. It's in my coat."

And she hadn't noticed it. "Meet me by the Christmas tree." She'd had to hide his gift because it wasn't wrapped in official color-coordinated wrapping paper.

Lexi was digging the purple package with the silver hologram ribbon out of the back branches of the tree when Spencer found her. She and Francesca had debated whether Lexi should get Spencer a gift, and if so, what it should be. Ultimately they decided she'd get him one, and if he didn't get her one, she could hold his for several days and call it a thank-you gift, which doubled as a reason to see him again.

A win-win investment, if she did say so herself.

"Seeing you play reminded me," he said, and handed her a small box wrapped in silver paper and cord.

Lexi had read enough women's magazines to be able to analyze the psychological meaning of a gift far beyond what any man intended. The fact that Spencer had brought her a gift at all was infinitely promising.

She opened the box to find a velvet sack. Inside were two brushed-silver sculpted hair clips. Stunning and exquisitely tasteful. "Spencer," she breathed his name as the gift-o-meter dinged a hit.

"I noticed that you always tuck your hair behind your ears, especially when you play. You have beautiful hair, and I was afraid you'd get irritated and cut it off one day if you couldn't keep it out of your face. So that's why I got you the clips. So you won't have to cut your hair."

Lexi gazed up into his handsome face. "They're beautiful." She would never cut her hair. Never, never, never.

Only, now she had to give her dorky gift to him. She reached into the tree branches and withdrew it.

"You got me a present?" A huge smile creased his face.

"It's just a…" Lexi trailed off as she watched him carefully unwrap the package so the paper wouldn't tear.

"Look at that!" He laughed as he pulled out an acrylic nameplate that had his name spelled out with resistors, capacitors, integrated circuits and other mysterious electronic parts embedded in the plastic.

"One of the art students made it for me," she explained. "Francesca and I like to support them when we can. I didn't notice that you had a nameplate."

"I don't." He grinned. "This is great. Thanks."

Lexi smiled, and tucked her hair behind her ears. "Oh, I do tuck my hair behind my ears! I didn't realize I did that so often. Let me put in the clips." She carried them over to the mirror hanging above the sofa. As she fastened them, she saw Spencer behind her. He was smiling as he studied the nameplate, and she breathed a sigh of relief.

Then he carefully smoothed the wrapping paper and ribbon, folded it and put it in his pocket.

Lexi's eyes stung as she realized that he probably hadn't been given many presents in his life, and her heart ached for the child within the man.

AT LAST, Christmas dinner with a real family. Spencer found he was actually a little nervous. He smiled down at Lexi, enjoying the sight of the clips in her dark hair, and followed her into the dining room.

They were just about to take their seats when Lexi's brother made his grand entrance. Everyone stared, which was obviously what he had in mind.

Les wore a red knit sleeveless undershirt that revealed his tattooed arms. Spencer had a hard time believing he was Lexi's twin. The guy acted more like he was Gretchen's twin.

"Leslie! Put on a shirt!" Mrs. Jordan's voice quivered with horror.

"I've got on a shirt."

"Put on a different shirt."

"Why?" He gestured to himself. "I kept to the color scheme."

"Lawrence, your son is not wearing a shirt."

"I see that." Lexi's father advanced purposefully toward his son. "Leslie, put on a shirt."

"Oh, I see what this is," Les said belligerently, and gestured to Emily. "She gets to show off her art, but *I* can't."

"Les, you have no art," Lexi said, "and don't pull that 'my skin is my palette' garbage, either."

"You mean you people are denying me my art *and* my lover?"

Spencer thought Lexi's mother would faint.

"And how does that make you feel?" Dr. Tracey asked.

"I'll tell you how it makes me feel. Worthless!"

Lexi audibly clamped her teeth together.

"I want to be accepted for who I am!"

"Les, nobody wants to accept your hairy armpits while we eat," Gretchen said, voicing everyone's opinion.

"Fine!" he snarled, and stomped off before he was forcibly escorted out by his irate father.

"More champagne while we await the return of my son?" Lawrence asked.

This suggestion was a hit with everyone, who eagerly held out their flutes.

A few minutes later, Les stormed back into the

room, his arms crossed over an unbuttoned shirt and Lexi's mother fixed a smile on her face. "Please be seated, everyone."

"At least Lexi and Gretchen were able to bring their *special* friends," Les complained, as the food was served. "For all I know, Arnaud is eating a frozen TV dinner."

Spencer looked down at Lexi questioningly. She lifted her water goblet and whispered, "Just keep smiling."

So Spencer smiled at Les.

Les raised his eyebrow and smiled back.

Oh, no.

Lexi reached her foot diagonally under the table and jabbed Les.

"W...e...l...l." Les never stopped looking at Spencer. "This could be the start of—"

"Les, cut it out," Lexi warned him.

"They named me Leslie. What do they expect?"

"Gravy, anyone?" warbled Lexi's mother. She'd worn her apron to the table where Spencer's turkey now reigned supreme.

Lexi's aunt smiled thinly. "You're so fortunate home-style potatoes are in fashion, Catherine. People will think the lumps are on purpose."

"You see? Whatever I do, it's criticized." Gretchen buried her face in her hands.

As Dr. Tracey patted Gretchen's back, she addressed the group at large. "Gretchen feels that her contribution of gravy isn't valued."

Catherine looked at Dr. Tracey as though she were an insect. "She's to be commended for accepting the blame for—"

"I would love some gravy, Mrs. Jordan," Spencer

said. "I'd been holding back because I know I've already taken more than my share."

"Then *you're* to be commend—"

"And, Mother, as long as you're passing dishes, I'd like more of the vegetable aspic," Lexi said.

"*A*spic!" Derek snickered.

"Yeah, *as*-pic!" echoed Melissa. "As-pic makes me si-ck, as-pic makes me si-ck," she sang, demonstrating that she'd inherited none of her mother's musical talent.

"Melissa!"

"Emily, I'll take care of it," Marshall said. "You must conserve your voice." He stood and reached across the table to take the aspic away from a surprised Lexi.

"Young lady," he said, plopping a spoonful on Melissa's plate. "You are to eat every mouthful of that."

"Noooo!" Melissa wailed.

"She'll throw up," Derek said, looking gleeful. "She knows how."

Spencer looked at the crying girl and believed him.

"Is *this* how you take care of the children?" Emily asked her husband.

"Yes, sweetheart." Marshall forced a spoon into the sobbing Melissa's hand. "While you're off crooning into the ears of sweating tenors, I'm raising our children."

"Only on the nanny's day off, *dear*."

"I hear resentment from you, Marshall," said Dr. Tracey.

"And speaking of sweating…" Les flapped his shirt.

"It *is* a trifle warm." Lexi's aunt Carolyn fanned herself. "The heat must be making my grandchildren cranky."

"Which *you* asked us to turn up to prevent Emily catching cold," Catherine pointed out smugly.

"Well, let's turn on the friggin' air-conditioning!" Les stood.

"We can't do that, Leslie," Catherine insisted.

"Then I'm going to be comfortable at Christmas dinner in my own home!" He jerked off his shirt and sat down. "Now, I'd like more turkey, dressing, potatoes *and* the gravy!"

Les reached his arm across the table to grab the dressing, which was in front of his aunt Carolyn.

She recoiled and Les saw her. "What's the matter? Can't you appreciate another person's art?"

"That's not a very good dragon," Derek said over Melissa's hiccuping wails.

Les stopped chewing and looked at his arm where a smeared dragon looked like it was crashing near the vicinity of his elbow.

Gretchen started laughing. "They're fake! Les's tattoos are fake!"

Dr. Tracey spoke, "Gretchen, rather than make fun of your brother, you should realize that he has been stripped of the mask he presents to the world. Use this opportunity to get to know the true person."

With a howl, Les bolted from the table.

Melissa threw up.

"So this is what I've been missing all these years," Spencer said to Lexi as her mother ran for the kitchen.

"Kinda brings a tear to your eye, doesn't it?" she said, and lifted her glass of champagne.

Carolyn was clucking over poor Melissa. "Don't worry about it, dear. It was the rich food." She helped the little girl down from the table as her parents tried to deal with the mess.

"Rich food!" Catherine had returned with paper towels in time to hear her sister's comment. "It was your son-in-law trying to choke his daughter!"

"Auntie Catherine isn't used to cooking for little people. Poor Auntie Catherine doesn't have any grandchildren of her own."

"And I'm not likely to get any!" Catherine gestured to Spencer. "After what he's seen today, I wouldn't blame Dr. Price for not wanting to marry into this family!"

"Mother!" Lexi visibly cringed.

Dr. Tracey stood. "I sense the repressed hostility in this family. You should all share your feelings with each other. I can offer you group rates."

In the midst of the babble that followed, Lawrence Jordan stood and gestured for Spencer to follow him. He glanced at Lexi.

"Go," she whispered. "Run for your life."

"I'll wait for you," he whispered back, and followed her father into the den.

"I see that in addition to rescuing dinner with a turkey, you came armed with a fine bottle of port, as well," Lawrence said, getting two glasses from the bar. "You are a man of rare talent and perception."

"Thank you, sir," Spencer said.

Lexi's father poured two glasses of port, handed Spencer one and gestured to a well-worn leather couch. "Now let's hear more about this mechanical hand of yours."

It was the opening he'd been waiting for. The opening he'd been preparing for. Even an average-size grant from this foundation would free him from the fund-raisers that annoyed the head of the Research Facility. It would keep the team together and let Spencer get back to design work.

And it was all within his grasp. Drawing a deep breath, Spencer began to pitch his project to Lawrence Jordan.

AFTER DR. TRACEY handed out her business cards, Emily and her family left, followed by Aunt Carolyn and a red-nosed Uncle Ben.

It occurred to Lexi that no one had been offered eggnog, yet the bowl was nearly half-empty. Gretchen tried to disappear up the stairs, but Lexi confronted her.

"You wanted the whole Christmas experience, so you can get yourself into the kitchen and help with the dishes."

"Excellent therapy, Gretchen." Dr. Tracey backed her up.

And it actually was. With Dr. Tracey's direction, the three women cleared the air and finished all the dishes, too. Dr. Tracey even persuaded a subdued Les to come downstairs with his pen-and-ink designs, which had been the basis for his tattoos. And, to be truthful, they were surprisingly good when they weren't displayed on sweating skin.

Lexi was also astounded to find out that Gretchen had been jealous of her all these years. And it wasn't surprising that their mother was jealous of her sister for giving birth to a musical prodigy.

Lexi was surprised to realize how much she'd sought her parent's approval, and was still doing so. She did feel smug in reporting her peace with Emily and how she wouldn't have wanted Emily's life.

Lexi hadn't meant to leave Spencer alone for so long, and had half expected him to have gone home. She went looking for him and found him in the den with her father. A football game was on the television, but the sound was barely audible.

What was audible was their conversation. Spencer was discussing the latest breakthrough on the robotic hand.

Lexi knew enough about the stupid hand to last her a lifetime, but she leaned against the doorway and listened for a moment, liking the way Spencer's face looked, its intensity as he discussed the project.

He'd even managed to interest her father.

Lexi wandered into the room and sat on the arm of the leather sofa where Spencer was seated. She was a little surprised to see all the rough drawings littering the coffee table, but she *had* been in the kitchen for a long time.

Spencer turned and smiled at her, but kept talking to her father. "And it was only after Lexi's roommate, Francesca, worked with us that I realized that there is a whole new area where the hand can be used."

Yeah, and what about me? Lexi thought, knowing she'd be horrified if he revealed *her* part in the hand's development to her father.

"Musicians. Think of the great artists who can no longer perform because of arthritis, or tendonitis or just plain weakness. Imagine giving them the means to continue to perform."

Very clever, Spencer, Lexi thought.

"It's the perfect marriage of science and the arts," her father said, looking more animated than Lexi had seen him look all day.

"It takes a man of vision to recognize that."

Maybe he was laying it on a touch too thick.

"I've always been considered a man who can discover new talent," Lawrence said.

"And so often unrecognized, I'll bet."

Lawrence nodded. "That's true."

"You're a better man than I am," Spencer said. "This has been years of my life, and I tell you, when we finally market the hand, I'm going to enjoy the recognition. Of course, I'll be sharing it with those who had the foresight to back me during the development phase."

Warning bells clanged. "Hey, Dad, we never got any of your eggnog," Lexi broke in.

"On the sideboard, honey. Now, how long will it be until you have a working prototype?" her father asked.

Lexi didn't like the way the conversation was going.

"We've got a rudimentary one now. As for a final version?" Spencer spread his hands. "Only time and money will tell."

"Spencer is a whiz at raising money, Dad. He has lots of backers—"

"Small backers. It would cut the administrative load significantly if we had to work with only one major source of funds."

"I can see that." Lawrence looked off into the distance.

"Spencer is going to help me think of fund-raising schemes for the music building at Littletree," Lexi said, not even trying to hide the desperation in her voice. "The old one is falling apart. We're losing prospective talent right and left. That's why I wanted to talk with you—"

"Alexandra." Her father held up his hand. "Spencer and I are discussing his robotic hand."

She looked at Spencer. He gazed back, wariness in his eyes.

He knew exactly what he was doing.

He'd known she was going to ask for funds for a new music building. While the accomplishment wouldn't be on Emily's level, being the driving force behind establishing Littletree as a music conservatory that turned out top-notch talent had been the way Lexi was going to make her mark in the music world.

All her warm fuzzies toward the poor little orphan boy evaporated. She felt cold inside and the silver clips he'd given her became heavy weights in her hair.

But with the coldness came great clarity. She may have been sidetracked in pursuit of her goal, but he'd never forgotten his. Rip had warned her.

This was the man known for his outrageous fundraisers, including one infamous calendar. And, like an idiot, she'd brought him to her father. Spencer had been telling her all along how important his project was to him, while she'd flung herself at him in leather underwear. She felt the humiliation burn in her face. She'd actually thought there might have been a chance for a relationship between them, but he'd only been stringing her along to get to her father.

Not only that, she and Francesca had provided him with the perfect justification to approach the Cultural Arts Foundation for money.

"You don't have much time before the end of the year, but I've got grant applications here in my desk." Her father was pulling open the file drawer. "I'd like to see an application from you if you're interested."

"Of course I'm interested," Spencer said, but he was looking at Lexi as he spoke.

The snake. The traitor. "As long as you're looking for forms, you might as well give me a set, as well," she said. "The Littletree music building needs to be razed. The situation is critical." She looked directly at Spencer as she spoke.

"That's more the jurisdiction of the board of regents, isn't it?" Spencer asked.

"I agree with Spencer," said her father.

"Then I'll give them the application," Lexi said.

"If you insist, sweetheart. Spencer, there will be a reception here on the twenty-eighth, honoring Mr. and Mrs. Robards and their houseguest." Frowning, he looked off in the distance. "Some pianist. Lexi's mother would know his name. However, since they've been major donors to both Littletree and to the foundation, all the foundation trustees as well as the regents should be in attendance." Lawrence handed a set of forms to each of them. "It would be beneficial for you to meet everyone. Perhaps you and Lexi can demonstrate the musical applications of the robotic hand."

No way.

"Lawrence?" called Lexi's mother. "Would you come to the kitchen? You really must see Leslie's—Les's art."

"If you two will excuse me?" her father asked.

Lexi barely noticed him leave. She stared hard at Spencer. "Don't apply to the foundation."

"Your father was very interested—"

"You knew I was going to ask my father for money for the music building."

"He didn't mention it." Spencer carefully folded the application papers and put them in the breast pocket of his jacket.

Lexi wanted to rip them out of his hand. "Because I haven't yet! The first time we met, I told you I wanted him to be in a good mood. That was why you were coming to dinner, remember?"

Something flickered in his eyes. "Actually, no, I didn't."

Could this person be the same man she thought she knew? "I don't believe you, and I don't believe what you've done. You have dozens of sources for funding. I don't."

His face was hard and determined. "Because I've spent years cultivating them."

"I don't have years. You saw the music building. It's falling apart. We're losing faculty. I'm even nervous about Francesca being up in Indiana. They've got a fabulous music department there and I'm afraid she'll apply for a faculty position."

"So why don't you apply, too?"

And that was the stake in the heart of their relationship, such as it had been. Talk about being suckered.

"Littletree has potential. I'm not giving up on it." She stood. He stood, too, looking as good as he ever had, darn it. "You'd better leave now."

11

"I'M TELLING YOU, Lexi, your strategy is all wrong."

"Francesca, didn't you hear me? Spencer Price got my father interested in that stupid hand project!"

They were in Francesca's room as she unpacked. Lexi had gone to the airport to pick her up, and the entire way home she'd ranted about Spencer's betrayal.

"I heard you all fifty times. You know why you're so angry?"

"Because he's going after my money?"

"You're angry because you found out he's going to apply for the grant before you slept with him. Now he's officially the enemy, and you think you *can't* sleep with him."

"Well, I can't!"

Francesca rolled her eyes.

"Can I?"

"You can, and you should." She zipped up her suitcase. "Look at you. You're all tense and worked up and angry, and it's not worth it."

"I happen to think our future at Littletree *is* worth it."

"Worth giving up Spencer Price?"

"I never had Spencer Price," mumbled Lexi.

"Which is my point. And the reception tonight is your chance to get him."

Frankie didn't expect her to show up there, did she? "I am *not* going to help him demonstrate that thing! And maybe my father is only being polite because he thinks Spencer and I are a couple. I'll tell him we've broken up."

"Wrong."

"Why?"

"You're missing a fabulous opportunity. You should go to the reception tonight."

"Again, why?"

"To keep him off balance. To distract him—even get him to leave with you before he can do any damage. He knows you're angry, right?"

"I hung up on him three times."

"He called you *three* times?"

"Maybe more. I only answered the phone three times."

"Very promising." Francesca pushed her suitcase under the bed and dumped her laundry in the hamper. "You're in a good position."

"For what?"

"Seducing him."

"I already tried that. Besides, he's a double-crosser. He no longer holds any attraction for me," Lexi said virtuously, though untruthfully.

"You'll need my help, of course." Francesca ignored her—as usual.

"You're telling me I should sleep with him for the sake of the music building?"

"If you actually need a reason to do what you want to do anyway, then that's as good a one as any. Now, we don't have much time." Francesca walked over to her lingerie chest and got out the velvet-lined box.

Lexi groaned. "Not the fake boobs."

"Lexi, you have an enhancement emergency."

Lexi was unaware that these sorts of emergencies existed.

"We want you to look hot—so hot that Spencer won't be able to tear his eyes away. So hot, he'll follow you as you lead him from the reception. He won't demonstrate the hand and your father will be ticked off. Bye-bye grant money. Go get the black knit dress—wait, get mine. It's smaller."

"Frankie—"

"Get my black beaded purse, too." She went to her nightstand and opened the drawer, withdrawing a foil packet.

"Francesca!"

Her roommate walked over to her and got the purse from the closet shelf herself. Opening it, she dropped in the packet. "Remember, your body is a temple, not an amusement park."

Lexi was enhanced enough to fall out of the dress. She was displaying a startling amount of manufactured cleavage, and parts of her body touched that had never touched before. Her center of gravity had shifted and she kept misjudging her personal space. She had to relearn how to walk because her normal healthy strides meant jiggles and there was a lot more to jiggle now.

She felt like a platter of gelatin.

She could only hope that her mother was so preoccupied she wouldn't notice Lexi's appearance.

The reception was in the music room. Even though Lexi was a few minutes early, people already milled about. She tried to stay out of sight until she could see whether or not Spencer was present. She saw her parents, another couple she assumed must be the honorees, the catering staff and couples her parents' age she thought might be the foundation trustees.

No Spencer as yet. This was good. She'd waylay him outside the door and he'd never even get to the reception.

"I didn't expect to see you here," said a familiar male voice behind her.

Lexi whirled around, forgetting her altered silhouette, and bounced against Spencer. "Hi, Spencer." She was too startled to try for the husky voice she'd practiced.

There was an arrested expression on his face as his gaze collided with her cleavage and stuck. She saw him swallow then meet her eyes with desperate determination.

Oh, cool. It was working. She smiled and held her shoulders back, feeling a little feminine flutter as his gaze flicked downward. "I hadn't planned to be here tonight."

"I know." Sweat beaded across his upper lip and she could actually see a vein throb in his temple. "I figured that Mushy Mischy guy would get you out."

"Mushy?"

"Yeah. Some piano guy."

That's right. Her father had said... Lexi gripped his arm. "Are you talking about *Mischa Wolfe?*"

Spencer nodded.

"Mischa Wolfe is coming here tonight?"

"So I was told." He raised the silver briefcase that held the hand. "I'm supposed to show him our friend, here."

Lexi nearly fainted. Mischa Wolfe—he of the flowing blond locks, smoldering eyes and high Slavic cheekbones—was in Rocky Falls and her mother hadn't bothered to tell her?

But she hadn't been answering the phone, had she? "Of course I want to meet him. I've been an admirer of his for several years." She couldn't resist adding, "You two have something in common. You've both done a calendar."

"Is that so?"

Lexi nodded. And jiggled. What? She'd have to watch facial movements, too?

The movement caught Spencer's attention. She saw him glance downward again. These things were almost as good as a hypnotist's swinging watch.

"Shall we go in?"

Lexi hesitated. That wasn't the plan, but she couldn't pass up a chance to meet Mischa Wolfe. Imagine, if she could get him to affiliate with Littletree… She shivered, another movement that Spencer watched with fascination.

Francesca should be here. Francesca was the perfect person to handle Mischa, and then Lexi could divert Spencer.

But only Francesca's breasts were here.

Lexi would have to make do. "Yes. Let's go in," she said to Spencer.

OH. MY. GOD.

Breasts. White skin. Breasts. Red lips. Breasts. Perfume. Breasts. Long black hair.

Lexi.

Lexi's breasts.

Oh. My. God.

Spencer swallowed. His mind wouldn't work. His legs barely responded.

And he'd thought he could just forget about her after he'd left on Christmas. She was angry with him, and he acknowledged that she had reason to be, but he'd been resigned to the fact that she was going to be another sacrifice in a long line of sacrifices he'd made to achieve his goals.

Now he wondered if he'd sacrificed too much.

They'd only been apart a few days, but everything about her seemed more intense than he'd remembered. Her lips were redder. Her hair was longer and blacker. Her eyes bluer. Her skin whiter. Her perfume more seductive. Her breasts more…more.

He couldn't stop staring at her as she moved around the room. He impressed no one at this reception. Sure, he spoke to many people. He must have smiled, because they smiled back at him, except for Lexi's parents who had frowned when they'd seen her.

But Lexi wasn't around to hear him discuss the hand—and he hoped he'd been discussing the hand—no, she was clinging to a man who looked like Lord Byron with a bleach job. Lexi seemed to find everything the man said wildly hilarious. She'd laugh, bending forward enough so that every male eye in the vicinity followed her movements.

No one was listening to Spencer talk about the hand. Even he didn't care about its applications for musicians. And he didn't like the piano dude. He didn't like the way he was looking at Lexi like she was his for the taking.

But she was, wasn't she? She was free. Spencer was free.

And he didn't like it.

LEXI COULD FEEL Spencer looking at her, though every man around was looking at her. Even her mother was looking at her, but that was in an entirely different way.

"I like Texas," Mischa said to her cleavage. "And I very much like Texas women. They are so healthy."

She was really tired of this whole breast thing, but if it got Mischa to Littletree... "I keep telling you that you'd love it here. And think, Littletree currently doesn't have an artist-in-residence." She gazed, or attempted to gaze into his eyes, but they so seldom met her own. "I could recommend you since I'm on the piano faculty." Like he'd need a recommendation.

"I am finding the concept of being artist-in-residence very attractive." He looked her up and down. "So much beauty and talent here." Holding out his hand, he said, "Come. Let us make beautiful music together."

Even from the flamboyant Mischa, the line was a howler, but Lexi smiled and gave him her hand. He led her across the floor toward the piano. "I would hear you play."

He wanted to evaluate the caliber of Littletree's faculty by listening to her. Lexi slipped Francesca's purse off her shoulder and set it beside her. This was a huge opportunity. If she impressed Mischa and he agreed to become Littletree's artist-in-residence, Lexi wouldn't need money from the foundation because the school trustees would fall all over themselves voting funds to upgrade the facilities. And it could happen. It was not rare for concert artists to lend their names to a small college, thus elevating it to premier status. It was the big fish in a small pond scenario. He'd gain stature, they'd gain stature, and he'd gain even more stature.

Spencer could have the foundation money with her blessing.

And with *that* stumbling block out of the way... She sought him out before she played. He was staring at her, his eyes dark, his jaw tight.

He was jealous, she realized. And he wouldn't be jealous if he didn't want her. The knowledge made her smile. It gave her hope.

And so there it was. The future all came down to Francesca's breasts and Lexi's playing.

As the crowd settled, Lexi was extremely conscious that she was preparing for one of the most important performances in her life. She'd pick something short and flashy—a crowd pleaser, because after all, they were in the middle of a cocktail party. Mischa would play too, she guessed. Probably Chopin, a favorite of his. For contrast, she ought to pick something modern, like Prokofiev.

Okay. This was it. But as Lexi crashed into the first chords, she knew she was in trouble. The stupid breasts were in the way. She couldn't sit at the right angle and her view of the keyboard was partially blocked. The driving rhythm coupled with the thundering chords meant there was serious jiggling going on that she could both feel and see. It distracted her, and her performance suffered.

Mischa stood right above her. Maybe with the view, he wouldn't pay as close attention to her playing. "Ah. One of my favorites," he murmured.

Yeah, she bet it was. Being in this situation was hideous and horrible and she'd never forgive Francesca.

She concluded the piece, mercifully without falling out of the dress, but it wasn't one of her more stellar performances.

Remembering to bow from the neck up only, Lexi acknowledged the polite applause and turned to Mischa, managing a smile. "And now it's your turn."

He inclined his head, kissed his fingers at her and took his place at the piano. The room hushed and Lexi knew her mother was thrilled that Mischa was going to play, especially after Lexi's miserable offering.

Rather than stand by his side, Lexi edged away from the piano. A half-dozen steps later, she backed into a warm body.

"I want to talk to you." Spencer's whisper tickled the side of her neck. "Where can we be alone?"

Lexi was still angry about her performance, which would have been fine if she hadn't been squeezed and uplifted for Spencer's benefit. So she wasn't feeling particularly charitable toward him right now. Beckoning with her head, she indicated that they should skirt the crowd and leave by a side door.

Mischa had begun a lengthy Chopin, so Lexi knew they had several minutes before he noticed she was gone. Getting Spencer away was her goal anyway, so she should be happy.

But she wasn't.

Mischa was going to make a pass at her, she knew. He'd been telegraphing it all evening. He was handsome and egotistical, true, but with justification. It would be so convenient to have an exciting affair with him—but Lexi wasn't interested, and the reason she wasn't interested was following her out of the music room.

Spencer.

He'd spoiled her for other men. Did he have to look so good? Did he have to be so smart? Did he have to act like such a rat?

Did she have to go and do something stupid like falling in love with him?

Love should have elevated her performance, considering what was at stake, but the only thing elevated was her chest. Nothing had changed. Spencer was still after the grant money, and Lexi should still try to lure him away.

The instant they were in the long hall outside the music room, Spencer pulled her into his arms. "Are you still mad at me?"

"Yes." She could be mad and in love at the same time, right?

He kissed her. Hard. "How about now?"

"Still angry."

He kissed her again. "I can keep doing this for as long as it takes."

And it just might work. "Why?"

"I want you."

It was exactly what he was supposed to say, which made her angrier. She didn't want him wanting her, she wanted him loving her. She glared at him. "You don't want me, you want my breasts."

"Okay. I want your breasts."

Forget the plan. Lexi couldn't stand it. "Then here." She reached inside the bodice of her dress and removed the squishy flesh-colored pads. "Take them. They're Francesca's and all they've done is cause a lot of trouble."

Then she stalked off toward the foyer.

SPENCER HAD NEVER been handed breasts in that way before.

All rational thinking stopped and he lost precious moments staring at them, absorbing the implications.

The slamming of the front door brought him out of his stupor. He started forward.

"Spencer!" Lexi's father hailed him.

Spencer quickly shoved a breast in each pocket and turned around.

"I've been looking for you. Now is the perfect time to demonstrate the hand. I confess that I'm anxious to see it in action, myself." Lawrence Jordan reached the doorway of the music room as applause sounded behind him. Looked like Mush-man had finished.

"I don't have a fully operational prototype as yet. We discovered a design flaw. Lexi, uh, helped with that, actually." Spencer swallowed. He had to go after her—now, if he ever wanted to patch things up between them.

Lawrence made a disgusted sound. "I see she's left, and after that abysmal performance, I don't blame her. And as for her appearance…" He drew a breath. "I hope you won't hold the actions of our daughter against us, Spencer."

Spencer was taken aback. "You should be proud of her."

Lawrence blinked. "Why?"

And with that one word, Spencer realized he knew more about what made Lexi tick than she did. No wonder she wanted money from her father's foundation—it would be tangible evidence of his approval. But it would also mean admitting that she couldn't achieve success without his help.

It was a tough spot to be in, and she must have known it, yet was willing to sacrifice her pride for something she believed in—the Littletree music department. Her project. Something as important to her as his was to him.

And he'd blown it for her.

He should be glad she hadn't slugged him on sight.

Squaring his shoulders, he looked her father right in the eye. "If you have to ask why you should be proud of your daughter, then you don't know her. I do. She's talented, smart, funny, ambitious and beautiful."

And you let her get away. What does that make you?

Lawrence smiled. "I see your folks raised you to be a gentleman. Sometimes parents try—"

"And sometimes they don't." Appalled at the man's attitude, Spencer cut him off. "If you'll excuse me?" He turned to leave.

"Where are you going? We're waiting for the hand demonstration."

"Sorry. Something more important came up." Some*one* more important.

"What could be more important than your presentation to the trustees?"

Spencer grinned. "I'm going to see a woman about a pair of breasts."

The look on Lawrence Jordan's face was worth torpedoing his chances.

He was halfway down the hall when she stepped out of the shadows. "Lexi! I was on my way to find you."

"You can't leave. You're supposed to demonstrate the hand to the trustees."

"I found something more important to do." It was hard to see her eyes in the shadowy light.

"I heard." She drew a shaky breath and he thought she might be near tears. "You can't—you shouldn't—oh, Spencer, I heard what you said to my dad. That was so…gallant!" Her voice broke on the word.

Spencer took her in his arms. "I meant it. All of it."

"But this is your big chance with the foundation!"

It was his big chance with her. "I don't want you hating me because I applied for the grant. It's all yours. Go for it."

"I don't hate you, and I'm not going to go for it," she said, and he heard defeat in her voice. "This evening, I realized my father would never approve a grant I applied for anyway. So now I'm not going to give him the satisfaction of knowing that I asked." She tossed her hair back. "But it's different for you. Come on. I'm not letting you waste this opportunity."

"Lexi—"

"And don't think I'm going to let Mischa demonstrate that hand. He'll just grab all the glory for himself."

"You're going to help me demonstrate the hand?"

She nodded. "That's why I came back."

And that's when Spencer knew he was in love with her.

It didn't hit him as hard as he thought it would, probably because he'd been falling for her since she'd first walked into his office. But it was still a jolt, and he had to find the right time to tell her. Soon.

MAKING A NOBLE SACRIFICE was great in theory, but Lexi found that reality was a bummer. Even though she knew that a working robotic hand would benefit more people than a new music building, she still felt a few pangs at giving up her hopes for a foundation grant.

If they'd rehearsed, she and Spencer couldn't have put on a better show. They pounded home the point that the invention was the perfect marriage of science and the arts.

And with Lexi's cleavage back to normal, she found Mischa Wolfe's interest in her had deflated, as well.

No loss.

Still, it was hard to watch Spencer as the center of attention and realize that all she had to look forward to was another year of declining enrollment, transferring faculty and clunky practice pianos.

Then there was Spencer, himself. Sure he'd said some nice things about her, but it wasn't a good idea to have the daughter of the foundation's chief trustee mad at you, was it?

Too bad he didn't realize Lawrence could not care less.

And with that depressing thought, Lexi slipped out of the reception.

12

LEXI CAUGHT FRANCESCA coming out of her bedroom. "You're back early. I haven't finished yet," her roommate whispered, looking around expectantly.

"Finished what?" Lexi snapped as she hung up her coat.

"Adding a little atmosphere to your room—where are my breasts?"

"With Spencer."

Francesca raised her eyebrows. "And where *is* Spencer?"

Lexi looked at her. "First tell me. Did you apply to Indiana?"

"What?"

"Did you apply for a faculty position at Indiana?"

Francesca held her gaze for a moment, then looked away.

"Frankie!" Fabulous. Great. Swell. Now she was going to lose the best roommate she ever had.

"It was only an application. What happened tonight?"

"Let's just say that right about now, the foundation is probably throwing all their money at Spencer."

Francesca collapsed against the doorjamb. "I can't believe the boobs didn't work."

"They worked." Lexi headed for her bedroom. "I just decided I didn't want them to anymore."

"Are you *crazy?*"

"No, I just wanted him to want me for me, and not—"

The doorbell interrupted her.

They stared at each other, then Francesca grinned. "And what was it you said you wanted?"

Lexi's heart was about to pound through her chest. "Don't answer that—"

But Francesca was already opening the front door. "It's about time you got here." She practically pulled Spencer inside.

He reached into his pockets. "I believe these are yours."

"There they are." Francesca breezily dropped the pads on the hall table. Pushing Spencer toward Lexi, she said, "She's in here."

Talk about unsubtle. Lexi cringed.

"Thanks." Spencer looked amused. "I see her."

Francesca smiled and kept pushing.

The only thing Lexi could do was back up all the way into her bedroom. "Frankie!"

"You two will want some privacy. Don't be shy, Spencer."

He gazed at Lexi. "I'm not."

Francesca pushed him through the doorway.

"Frankie." This was completely mortifying. Even more so when Lexi saw her bedroom. Francesca had draped scarves over the lamps, replaced Lexi's practical cotton sheets with satin ones and must have spread around and lit every candle they owned for atmosphere.

"I'm on my way out the door. I'm going to the lab.

We're planning our New Year's Eve party. I did mention we were having one here, didn't I?"

"No." Lexi glared at her.

"Well, we are." She looked at her watch. "I won't be back for at least two hours. Bye." She closed the door.

Spencer looked like he was struggling not to laugh.

"She—I—"

The door opened. "Me, again." Francesca tossed something at Lexi. "You left your purse on the hall table." She smiled at Spencer. "We're trying to cut back on the clutter. Bye."

Lexi stared at the purse she'd borrowed from Francesca, until she heard the front door slam. "Subtlety has never been one of my roommate's strengths," she said into the silence.

"Or mine." He stepped forward, took the purse out of her hands and set it on the bedside table. Drawing her to him, he said, "I'm in love with you. You want to talk about that now, or later?"

Lexi's mouth dropped open.

"Later, it is. Excellent choice." He leaned forward. She put her hand on his chest, his gloriously, over-clothed chest. "Wait a minute, wait—a—minute." Gesturing to the room, she said, "This is all Francesca's doing. Even the breasts were her idea."

He moved his arms around her. "She has good ideas."

"But that's not me!"

"And you think I don't know that?" He looped his arms around her. "But I have to point out that some of it's you. Remember, I've seen you play the piano. Your face…" He exhaled. "I hope I can create those expressions." Smiling down at her, he added, "I intend to try. Soon." His fingers reached for the zipper at her back.

He loved her. He said he did, but… A tiny sound escaped Lexi's throat.

"What's the matter now?"

"If you're only here for a hot celebratory fling, then forget it."

He drew back, looking puzzled. "Didn't I tell you I loved you? I meant to."

"Yes, but you can't just tell a woman you love her out of the blue."

"Why not? I wanted you to know as soon as I figured it out." He looked extremely pleased with himself. "Actually, I knew it right before the demonstration, but you left before I could tell you. And once I knew I loved you, then I could see that you loved me, too."

"That is so egotistical."

"But true?"

"But true," she admitted, and watched him smile. She smiled, too.

He unzipped her dress. "So, is the fling still on?"

"Spencer! If you really love me, then we've got a lot to talk about."

"We've only got two hours. I can talk and undress you at the same time." He pulled her dress off her shoulders. "You can talk and undress me at the same time."

"You're not going to be listening."

He dropped a kiss onto her shoulder. "Probably not."

And as he worked his way across her collarbone

and up the side of her neck, Lexi figured that she wasn't going to be doing much talking.

He peeled her dress away, exposing the deflated bra. And how sexy was that? She crossed her arms over her chest. "There's...not as much there as you were expecting."

"Anything more than a mouthful is a waste," he said, unhooking the bra and tugging it out from under her arms.

She still kept her arms crossed, in the grip of an unexpected attack of shyness. She hadn't been shy with the leather underwear; why now?

Spencer only smiled and reached behind her, gathering her hair and bringing it over her shoulders to cover her. "A fantasy of mine," he explained.

He gazed at her, letting her see the heat of his desire. Lexi felt an answering warmth growing within her, melting away the shyness.

Leaving her hair in place, she dropped her hands. "You're wearing too many clothes."

"I wondered when you'd notice."

She stepped toward him and unknotted his tie, dropping it in a silken pool next to the bed. "We might need this later."

"Ah, later. Before we go any further, I've thought of something else we'll definitely need. I wasn't expecting to see you tonight—"

"In the purse." She pointed to the beaded bag on the nightstand.

He raised his eyebrows.

"Francesca," Lexi explained.

Spencer slowly smiled. "I like your roommate." He helped her with the buttons on his shirt. "A lot."

"She has her moments." And Lexi didn't feel even the tiniest pang of jealousy.

"And you definitely have yours." He shrugged out of his shirt.

There was his chest. The calendar chest. In full, living color. She spread her hands across his skin, feeling the warmth, feeling his heart beat. "This is much better than the picture."

He laughed, the rumbles vibrating against her hands. "I love watching your face. It's so expressive."

"Is it?" she asked absently, and kissed him near his heart. Resting her lips against his skin, she could feel his pulse.

He splayed his hands over her naked back and she smiled when his heart rate accelerated.

She lifted her face and he kissed her forehead, each eyelid and her nose before lightly taking her lips. "I've never made love to a woman before," he whispered against her mouth.

"What?" That startled her.

"I've never told a woman I loved her." The look he gave her managed to be both tender and hot. "Therefore, I've never made love."

Ever the scientist. "You're doing just fine."

He ran his hands over her hips. "I intend to do better than fine." And he kissed her as he'd never kissed her before, exploring her mouth with a sensual confidence that made her knees week.

I've hit the big time, she thought just before she couldn't think anymore. When his hands began to move over her skin, her knees gave out.

She flung her arms around his neck to keep from falling, but her sudden movement sent them tumbling backward onto the bed covered with Francesca's peach satin sheets.

The fabric was cool and slick against her back. She was pillowed in softness and covered in Spencer, who continued to kiss her. All in all, a good position to be in.

He laced their hands together. Stretching her arms wide, he lifted himself to one side, then gently blew the strands of hair off her chest.

"That tickles."

He smiled. "Tickles good, or tickles bad?"

"Tickles with potential."

His smile faded and he turned serious. "That's what I see for us, Lexi. Potential. I never thought I'd find a woman like you, and even then, I thought it would be years before I could take the time to love her. I thought I had to be somebody first. But with you, I'm already somebody."

She felt the same way and only now realized it. "We're both trying to prove something. I'm trying to get out from under Emily's shadow, and you want to show up those kids from your boarding school. But with each other, we don't have to prove anything."

"Oh, I don't know." He released her hands and tugged off her shoes. "I wouldn't mind proving my exceptional prowess as a lover."

She was surprised into a laugh even as his words sent a thrill through her. "All right. Prove it."

He gave her a heavy lidded look. "Gladly."

Levering himself off the bed, he slowly and deliberately finished undressing.

The flames from a dozen candles caressed his body with a warm light.

The flames from a dozen candles weren't one-tenth as hot as his dark gaze. It scorched its way over her body, leaving her mouth dry.

He was perfectly gorgeous with sculpted muscles and flawless proportions. And he was hers. All hers.

She sat up, swung her legs over the side and stood, preparing to undress, too, but he shook his head.

"Let me." He knelt and kissed her stomach before pulling off her slip. He made quick work of the panty hose—quicker than Lexi usually did, until all she was wearing were the white cotton panties Francesca scorned.

But between his mouth and his hands, Spencer made even white cotton sexy.

And then they were gone, too.

"I've dreamed of seeing you like this," he whispered. "Dressed only in your hair." Then he drew it away and put it behind her shoulders. "You're beautiful."

"You make me feel beautiful." She gave in to temptation and pressed herself against his body, reveling in the feel of skin against skin.

His sigh echoed hers, and they stayed in each other's arms for long moments. Then with a groan, he pressed urgent kisses against her mouth, her neck and her breasts.

They tumbled back onto the bed with the sheets as cool as their lovemaking was hot.

For Lexi, it was more than making love, it was feeling completely accepted as she was by another human being. It wasn't something she'd been aware of craving until the need was filled.

But that's what Spencer's touch did—it drew out

emotions she'd never before experienced. His every caress demonstrated the depth of his feelings for her. The awe on his face was as seductive as his mouth and his restrained desire was as arousing as the stroking of his fingers.

He was very much a man, and made her feel like that much more of a woman. Even watching as he opened Francesca's purse did nothing to mar the image. His caring and his love nearly made her weep.

And when he joined with her, she did weep, her emotions at the breaking point.

"Hush, love," he whispered, kissing her temple, smoothing her hair.

"It's so... I feel..."

"I know. Me, too." And he began to move, carrying her with him, urging her onward with whispered endearments, until she shuddered, moaning his name. Seconds later, he gasped, "Lexi!" and she clutched him as his tremors rocked them both.

She never wanted to move, never wanted to break the spell that bound them together. When he tried to pull away, she gripped him harder.

"I'm not going anywhere." He gazed down at her with a possessiveness that thrilled her. "I never want to be with another woman, and I can't stand the thought of you with another man. Marry me." It was a demand, giving her no choice.

Not that she wanted one. "Yes."

LONG AFTERWARD, as she lay with her head pillowed against his chest, Lexi thought to ask about the demonstration. "You had to have left right after I did. I hope you didn't tick off the trustees."

"I said everything that needed to be said. Mush man actually helped."

"His name is Mischa."

She felt him smile. "When the trustees started talking specific dollar amounts, I told them that while you and Francesca had graciously worked with us, for full-scale development of a robotic hand suited to the particular needs of musicians, I'd have to affiliate with a university that had better facilities to test it. Otherwise, I'd have to decline any offers of funding and concentrate on our original medical applications."

"You turned down the money?" She tilted her head until she could see his face. "Are you crazy?"

"It was never actually offered. But that's when Mush—Mischa pretty much trashed the Littletree music department, I'm sorry to say."

Lexi frowned. "I didn't think my performance was *that* bad."

Laughing, Spencer dropped a kiss on the top of her head. "He'd toured the building with the Robards. Let's just say he was underwhelmed."

Lexi drew her breath between her teeth. "I didn't know he'd already seen the building. How embarrassing. I was trying to get him to consider being our artist-in-residence in hopes of prying money out of the board of regents. Oh, well. Scratch that."

"I don't know. There were a lot of red faces in the crowd. That's when I left. But you may come out of this better than you thought."

"Speaking of red faces... Francesca should be back soon. We ought to get dressed."

Spencer began tracing ever-widening circles on

Lexi's shoulder. "She doesn't strike me as the type of woman who is easily embarrassed."

"She's not."

"Then there's no reason for us to get out of this bed, is there?"

She smiled. "I can't think of a single one."

"In that case," he said, shifting beneath her, "how would you like eggs for breakfast?"

"THIS IS THE BEST New Year's Eve party we've ever had." Francesca drifted back into the kitchen and opened another bag of chips. "The male-female ratio is killer. Bob and Gordon have fixed the VCR and Dan and Steve are working on the stereo hookup for the big-screen TV we rented."

"It's the only New Year's Eve party we've ever had," Lexi told Spencer.

He murmured something, smiled and kissed her. They'd been doing a lot of that lately.

"Are the fajitas ready yet? The guys are hungry."

Lexi and Spencer were in charge of assembling the condiments, but had gotten into an argument over the seasoning for the guacamole and had been kissing and making up ever since.

"You haven't even put out the sour cream! I'm convinced that love makes people worthless for anything else," Francesca said in disgust.

"Speaking of, Murray called and said he was on his way."

"Oh? Isn't he here?" Francesca asked with elaborate casualness. "I hadn't noticed. Rip and I have been star gazing."

Spencer grinned at Lexi. "Murray had to stop by

the chemistry department chairman's party. He was in charge of dry ice."

"Well, *I* don't care if he prefers that party to ours," Francesca said with a toss of her head.

"Frankie, it's only eight o'clock. He'll be here."

As if on cue, the doorbell rang, followed by knocking. In spite of her professed indifference, Francesca practically ran to the door.

"Spencer!" Murray burst in. "I just found out— whoa." He'd seen Francesca.

Lexi happened to know that she was wearing the heavy artillery—her tiger cat suit—and she was regarding Murray like a predator.

"Happy—" That was as far as he got before she kissed him.

"I better bring him up for air," Spencer said. "Hey, Murray, what were you going to say?"

Francesca released him and he blinked. "Say? Oh. When I got to the party, they were all talking about the grant and the music building redo."

"What?" Lexi and Spencer asked in unison.

"Yeah, it was just voted on and a couple of the regents were there. Have you heard anything?"

"No," Spencer said, shaking his head, when there was a knock against the still-open door.

"I think I can shed light on the mystery," said a familiar voice.

Lexi stared. "Mom and Dad?"

"Happy New Year, Alexandra." Her mother kissed her on both cheeks. "Lawrence?"

Her father smiled the widest smile Lexi had ever seen from him. "We thought we'd run into you and Spencer at the Wainright Inn, but you aren't playing tonight."

"No," a bemused Lexi said.

"We must get back there, but we wanted to give you this first." Lexi's father withdrew an envelope and handed it to Spencer.

He ripped open the letter and looked stunned. "It says the foundation is awarding us a continuing grant subject to the refurbishment of the Littletree music facilities."

"I don't believe it." Lexi leaned over and read the words—twice—and they still didn't sink in. "They're going to redo the building?"

"The regents voted this afternoon," her father confirmed.

"About time," Francesca said, and led Murray to the den.

"This is…this is…" Wordlessly, Spencer shook his head.

Lexi knew exactly how he felt. Now he could forget raising money and get back to doing what he loved.

"Alexandra, I want you to know how pleased and proud I am that you had the vision to see the applications of Spencer's hand," her father said. "You demonstrated the sort of forward-thinking I'd always hoped my children would have. Well-done."

Spencer had slipped his arm around her waist and now he squeezed her gently.

"You should hear your father." Catherine looked up at him fondly. "He's been quite a bore going on about you two."

Lexi smiled. A month ago, she would have been elated. Now, while her father's approval pleased her, she would have felt the same without it. And it was all because of the man at her side.

Her parents stayed a few more minutes, meeting Spencer's team, and then went on to their party at the Wainright Inn.

"Looks like we're both going to be busy next year," Spencer said, closing the door after her parents and sliding his arms around her waist.

"But not too busy to be together."

"And we'll have to work a wedding in there, too."

Lexi gripped him hard. "Oh, Spencer, I do love you."

He grinned. "I know."

Epilogue

From the spring issue of Texas Men...

MARVELOUS MATCHES

Ladies, better hurry if you're waiting to write to the Science Hunks featured in our fall issue. We already have an engagement! Yes, lucky Alexandra Jordan has nabbed Mr. December, Spencer Price. That's a photo of the happy couple at the top of this column. Also reporting in is Murray Bendel, who is seriously dating a cellist, and requests that you hold your letters.

But there are plenty of other eager Texas men featured in this issue. Why don't you call us for their addresses and maybe you'll be featured in our next "Marvelous Matches" column!

Until summer, this is Tonya for *Texas Men*.

Question: How do you find the
red-hot cowboy of your dreams?

Answer: Read on....

Texas Men Wanted! is a brand-new
miniseries in Harlequin Romance®.

Meet three very special heroines who are all looking for
very special Texas men—their future husbands! They've all
signed up with the Yellow Rose Matchmakers. The Yellow
Rose guarantees to find any woman her perfect partner....

So for the cutest cowboys in the whole state of Texas,
look out for:

HAND-PICKED HUSBAND
by Heather MacAllister in January 1999

BACHELOR AVAILABLE!
by Ruth Jean Dale in February 1999

THE NINE-DOLLAR DADDY
by Day Leclaire in March 1999

Available wherever
Harlequin Romance books are sold.

Catch more great

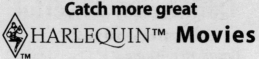

HARLEQUIN™ Movies

featured on **the movie channel** tmc

Premiering December 12th
Bullets Over Boise
Based on the novel by bestselling author Kristen Gabriel

Don't miss next month's movie!
Premiering January 9th
At the Midnight Hour
Starring Patsy Kensit and
Simon McCorkindale
Based on the novel by bestselling
author Alicia Scott

If you are not currently a subscriber to The Movie Channel, simply call your local cable or satellite provider for more details. Call today, and don't miss out on the romance!

the movie channel tmc   **HARLEQUIN®**
                                    Makes any time special ™

100% pure movies.
100% pure fun.